PACESETTERS

EVBU MY LOVE

HELEN OVBIAGELE

ISBN: 978-1-957076-91-1

NEO BOOKS

Contents

Chapter 1

Evbu sat alone at a table near the window in the Ikeja International Airport departure lounge and stared at the planes perched like great birds on the tarmac. She was smartly dressed the Senegalese way in wide white trousers, black and white agbada in adire and a matching head-tie worn high. She wore large gold hoop earrings and matching bracelets. Her make-up was subtle. The total effect was one of elegance, evoking many admiring glances, but she was deep in thought in that noisy room and was oblivious of any attention she was drawing to herself.

Suddenly, there was a lull in the conversation which brought Evbu out of her reverie. The cause of the hush was the entrance of a distinguished-looking elderly man, trailed by an entourage of about eight people, each carrying a small piece of luggage. As he caught sight of Evbu he let out a small cry and walked as rapidly as his weight would permit him towards her. Evbu stiffened. The man's face looked quite familiar, but for a second she could not put a name to it. He drew near with an outstretched hand.

'Evbu, my dear! It's been a long, long time.' He was a bit taken aback when she did not respond immediately. 'Don't tell me you don't recognise me anymore, Evbu! Surely, it was not all that long ago that you were with me?' It all came back to her then.

'Chief, oh Chief!' she exclaimed, jumping to her feet and seizing his still outstretched hand. Most of the people in the lounge were now openly watching them, and the Chief looked round triumphantly, en- joying the kind of attention he was getting.

'Evbu, you naughty girl. You never bothered to ask of me since you left."

'I'm sorry, Chief. What with one thing and the other, I just couldn't find the time. And I knew that you were always away on business trips.'

'You look as lovely as ever. Didn't you recognise me just now, or were you just pretending not to know me?'

'Oh, no, I could never do that. It was just that you looked so much younger than when I last saw you," she lied. If anything, the Chief was much fatter and rounder and she had wondered who the bloated stranger was. 'How's the family, Chief?'

Just as he was about to reply, a huge and fearful- looking middle-aged woman came into the room with five people and made her way to where Evbu and the Chief were standing. The Chief saw her and then stammered, 'My dear, you, you remember Evbu, don't you? She used to...' The woman did not allow him to finish.

'I don't remember her at all,' she said in a loud voice. "Who is she?"

'Good evening, madam,' said Evbu politely, coming forward. 'Hello,' the woman replied curtly. 'Look Chief, I'm tired of standing about, let's go and sit over there. She indicated a table that was at the far end of the room. 'Come on, come on," she added, edging him away.

'Yes, my dear,' said the husband meekly, and without a backward glance at Evbu, waddled after his wife. Evbu sat down feeling rather humiliated. Some people shot pitying glances at her, but she stared back boldly and they quickly left her alone. Now, she was amused. It was quite obvious that the Chief was still very much afraid of his wife. Yet when he was away from her he was a different person-all full of confidence and authority. Oh, well, people have many sides to them.

'Will passengers for USAIR Flight 342 for New York, please proceed to the aircraft,' came a voice over the loudspeaker. 'This is the final announcement.'

Evbu glanced around anxiously. Steve should have come back ages ago. He had left to escort her mother, brother and sisters back to their car. They had come all the way from Benin City to see Steve and Evbu off, but she had not been able to see them to the car herself because she knew she would break down. The parting had been painful.

She picked up her vanity case and Steve's jacket and began to walk towards the exit. As she passed by the Chief's table, she pointedly ignored the wife, shook hands boldly with him and bade him 'Good- bye'. Out of the corner of her eye she could see the woman fuming. Evbu was a bit surprised at herself. Several years ago she would not have thought such behaviour becoming of a lady, but she had learnt over the years to give as good as she got and much more if she could.

She joined the queue at the door but kept an eye on the other door for Steve. Suddenly she saw him striding towards her, gently pushing people aside, his eyes holding hers all the way. Then he was at her side with a protective arm thrown round her. She shut her eyes and put her head briefly on his shoulder. 'Oh, Steve, where would I be without you?'

'I love you baby,' he whispered in her ear as they went through the door and got into the bus that was to take them to the aircraft.

As they drove through the night, she looked back at the receding airport buildings and wondered when and if she would ever see Lagos and Benin City again. She shivered from the cool night air and snuggled up to Stove, who held her close. This was not her first trip abroad. In fact, she had been to Europe several times and once to the United States, but this journey was different, quite different.

Yes, what she felt for him was unlike anything she had felt for any man so far in her life; no aching heart, just love and the confidence that she was loved in return. Her life now seemed to have a sense of direction, some purpose.

Chapter 2

She had been born the third of a family of five children and was called 'Evbu' which meant 'dawn' in Edo dialect because she had been born very early in the morning. Her father had been a farmer in Isi, but when she was five he had moved the family to Benín City where he got a job as a labourer at the aero-dome. Through hard work and devotion, he later rose to the rank of a supervisor.

When she left Primary School at the age of sixteen, Evbu's father was in favour of her getting married right away before she became too old. Evbu would have preferred to go to Secondary School like some of her friends, but she knew that that was out of the question. Owing to financial difficulties even her brothers, who had left school some years before, were not able to go to Secondary School. One was working as a clerk at the Public Works Department.

The other was a pupil-teacher at an Infants' School. The boys were very ambitious and had begun to study for G.C.E. examinations.

They spent half their salaries on overseas tuition. Their father was due to retire shortly which would mean less money in the house. Already, workers at the airport had been told that the authorities intended to make use of farming land for the extension of the new runway. This meant that there would be no more income from the farm. It was decided that Evbu should work as a shop assistant in a chemist's shop which belonged to Mr Osunde, her mother's cousin. Mr Osunde was very willing to have Evbu work for him because he knew that, being pretty, she would draw more customers and, because she was related to him, he could pay her less than his other workers and still have her loyalty.

Evbu enjoyed working at the shop because in between serving the customers she had time to read novels and magazines. She was an avid reader. The other girl in the shop, Clara, used to tease her about her addiction to books.

'Hm, if you read so much, Evbu, you will have no man to marry you,' she told her one day.

'Why not? Anyway, I don't care. One day, I will have saved enough money to go abroad and study. Then I can look after myself when I qualify and not depend on any man.'

"That's fine,' laughed Clara, 'but you will get married. Look at the way Osaretin, that teacher, runs after you. Do you think he will let you out of his sight to go abroad?'

'Osaretin! What makes you think he is interested in me of all people? He comes here for you, I'm sure.' 'Ha! so you think! The other day he was asking me what colour of dress you like best, so that he could go and buy some material for you.'"

'Really, that is a surprise! Why is he interested in me now, when he used to thrash me so much? I remember clearly that whether I offended him or not, he would detain me at break and give me extra work to do. I quite hated him then. I'm only polite to him these days because I thought he was your boyfriend. Moreover Uncle Osunde has warned me that it is important to please people who come to the shop.' 'Anyway, there it is! He is crazy about you. 'But he is too old for me! He must be about forty or more. He once told me that he could remember the day I was born."

'He is not old,' said Clara, who was in her early twenties. 'I think he is about 32 or 33. He has been busy studying all these years. That is why he is still unmarried. It is the desire of many mothers in Ogbe to have him wed one of their daughters. He is not bad- looking and he is well-respected.*

'Well, good luck to all of you. I'm not interested. When I make up my mind to have a boyfriend, I will have one nearer my own age who will be interested in the things I'm interested in.

'Ha! ha! Those books you read have affected the way you think. Fancy any girl refusing Osaretin! I suppose you are waiting for a great romance like in the stories you read. Life is not like that I can tell you. If you take a look at the marriages around you, you will agree with what I have said. Which of the boys who come to see you do you fancy, then?'

'No one as yet. What about you?'

'Nobody special yet. But I really like Osaretin. It's no use though since he has eyes only for you. He would make a nice steady husband and he is not too old for me.

'Don't you want to study further?' asked Evbu. 'Study? Oh no! Primary Six is enough for me. I just want to get married and settle down."

During the following months Evbu came to realise that Osaretin was really interested in her. He called at the shop and at the house regularly. He began to help her brothers with their studies. One day he left a parcel with her mother for her. In it she found a nice pair of shoes and some pink material. She liked these things but she did not want to accept them because she was not prepared to commit herself. He might think that his affection was returned. Her mother was surprised at her reaction.

'Goodness, Evbu, why do you want to return these things? This is Osaretin's way of saying that he wants to court you.'

'Well, I don't want him to court me. He is too old for me."

'Old! I don't think so. He was less than your pre- sent age when you were born. Don't you like him?'

'I like him, but I don't love him.'

'What's the difference? You need someone who will be able to take care of you. He has a nice steady job and he is young."

'I will marry a man I'm really in love with like you did. Look at the way Papa still cares for you and you for him after all these years!"

"That's true. I agree that your father and I were very much in love in our own way in Isi, but the real love and caring established itself through the years in the things we shared together.'

'I will wait, Mama, until I find a man I really know I care about. Not just anyone that others feel is suitable for me. I don't mind if it takes a hundred years."

'Please yourself, Evbu. No one will force you to marry against your wish. The oracle man told us when you were born that you must be allowed to choose your husband. If you do not like Osaretin, that's alright. There will be others. It's just that your father and I thought that...

'Never mind what you and Papa think about Osaretin, Mama,' said Evbu, cutting in. 'God will guide me to the right man.

'Amen!'

Evbu returned the things, but Osaretin was not discouraged. She was the prettiest girl around and he always liked the best for himself. All his life he had wanted to excel at things in order to show his father, who had deserted the family when Osaretin was very young, that he had succeeded without his help. Of all his father's sons, he had so far achieved the most.

He was now a Grade II teacher and very shortly he might be made headmaster of a small school somewhere else in Benin City. He knew he could have his pick of girls, but his dearest wish was to have Evbu for his wife. Evbu was bound to produce nice, healthy, good-looking children for him. She had been one of the most intelligent girls who passed through his school, but she always seemed to be in a world of her own. She had always seemed oblivious to men's admiration for her, even when she was at school.

Then he thought it was pride. That was why he had tried to subdue her by caning and detaining her at break time. Evbu was amazed that after she returned Osaretin's gifts he intensified his advances. He brought her books to read, but not the type she liked. They were serious books dealing with philosophy and politics. She did not read them. After some time she got used to his presence at home and at the shop. Clara had left to get married and another girl, Itota, had taken her place. Itota was also full of Osaretin's praises and Evbu began to think that there might be something in what everyone was saying and she might do well to marry him. She consented to go out with him. He took her on his motorcycle to neighbouring villages for cultural shows and festivals and they visited famous and historical places. They went to watch plays and films too. Although she was not in love with him, she was proud to be in his company because he seemed to be known and respected everywhere they went. Clearly, he was very popular.

Just before Christmas, Osaretin went to her father to ask formally for Evbu's hand in marriage. Her father called her in and asked if she wanted to marry Osaretin and she agreed. Two weeks later they were engaged. Her father asked only for a small bride price. He said that no daughter of his was going to be sold like a cow. He had been relieved and happy when Evbu had said that she would marry Osaretin. He had always admired the young man's determination to succeed in life and was also grateful to him for the help he was giving to his sons in their studies. He was proud to have him for a son-in-law. The wedding, by native law and custom, was fixed for June the following year when Evbu would have saved enough money to buy all she needed for her trousseau.

As soon as he had paid the dowry, Osaretin regarded Evbu as his property. He took to calling at the shop and the house any time he liked. On Saturdays he would spend most of his time at the shop, scrutinising all the men who called in. Every evening he would call to take her home. At first Evbu was amused by his possessiveness and even enjoyed it, but after some time it began to annoy her. While Itota kept telling her how lucky she was that he cared for her that much, she felt stifled. She could not help thinking that if he behaved like that when they were married she would run away, and repay the dowry later.

One day, just before Easter, two boys came into the shop. Evbu recognised one of them, Henry, as a brother of a former classmate of hers, but the other boy, tall, good-looking and trendily dressed in tight- fitting trousers, was a complete stranger to her. Her heart missed a beat when she looked up and met his eyes. His eyes looked at her over hungrily and she blushed.

'Hello, Evbu,' greeted Henry familiarly, 'how are you and how is our dear teacher?' She laughed. Fine, thank you. I didn't know you were back in town. Is Ehi here too? I understand she is doing very well at Queen's College."

'Oh, she is alright. In fact, she should be here this evening. We should have travelled together yester- day, but she made an excuse and stayed behind. I'm sure it has to do with her new boyfriend.'

"There you go again. You are always jealous of her boyfriends. Please tell her that I will call to see her tomorrow evening on my way home. Now, what can we do for you? This is Itota, my colleague. She replaced Clara."

'Hello,' said Itota to both boys.

Hello, Itota. I'm pleased to meet you. I understand that Clara left to get married. Could we have some aspirins, please?" me.'

'Henry.' said his friend, 'you've not introduced

'Oh, sorry. Evbu, Itota, meet my friend Jide Jones. We call him "Double J". We are both in the same class at King's College,' he winked. 'He is here to spend the holiday with me.'

'Hello, Evbu. Hello, Itota." 'Hello,' chorused both girls.

The boys bought their aspirins and left soon after- wards.

"That's a pretty girl,' observed Jide on the way. A real cool, dark and stately beauty!"

'You mean Itota?'

'You know who I mean. I noticed that you did not want to introduce me to her.'

"There were two girls there. How did I know that you wanted to be introduced to one of them?'

"There was only one girl there as far as I'm concerned. The tall, ebony-black, well-shaped one. She seems utterly unaware of how sensational she looks. No make-up, nothing. Did you notice the gorgeous eyes?'

'Yes, I did, Casanova. But please, hands off. She is engaged to my old teacher and she's quite a decent girl. I've always been crazy about her myself, but have never had the courage to tell her so.'

'Okay, I merely made an observation. Gosh, she really is something! I didn't know there were pretty Edo girls.'

'Hm, don't let Ehi hear you say that. She thinks that Edo girls are the prettiest in the world."

Imagine how nice it would be kissing those lips." 'Goodness, Jide! Hearing you talk, one would think that you were a sailor seeing a dame for the first time on land in two years. You've got numerous girls in Lagos to keep you happy, surely."

So have you, old boy! What's wrong in admiring a pretty girl? She's great.

'Please yourself, but I don't think you have a chance in hell with her. She is already engaged to be

'Oh. I can always dream. There's no harm in that, is there?' married.'

'None whatsoever! Now, let's hurry up if we intend to go to the pictures after supper."

From then on Evbu thought about Jide most of the time. Why had he insisted on being introduced? Was he interested in Itota or in her? There was no doubt that she was infatuated with him herself. How else could she explain the way she thought constantly and romantically about him. She told herself to stop being ridiculous.

A fabulous boy like that was bound to have lots of girlfriends in Lagos. Besides, she was already engaged to be married. Her bride price had been paid and all that was left was for her to move into her husband's house. Well, she could always have her dreams.

A week later, Jide walked into the shop alone, while Itota was out for lunch. The girls took it in turns to go for lunch.

'Hello, Evbu. Remember me?"

'Hello,' said Evbu, flattered that he remembered her name.

'Oh, yes! How are Henry and Ehizogie?'

'Fine, I suppose. They went to see their uncle at Uzebu, so I thought I would come and chat with you.'

Evbu smiled, not quite knowing what to say. Perhaps he was interested in her. After all, he had not asked for Itota yet.

'Itota is out for lunch,' she said. 'She should be back quite soon."

'Who's Itota? Oh, you mean the other girl here? I haven't come to see her,' he said, staring straight in- to her eyes. 'I have come to see you. I would have come earlier, but Henry kept warning me to keep away from you because you are engaged to be mar-ried. But I can't keep away any longer."

Evbu was amazed at his direct approach. Most boys who had approached her had taken weeks and sometimes months to come to the point of their visits. She did not know what to say.

'I would like you to be my girlfriend,' he added after a short silence.

'I can't! I'm as good as married.'

'Don't you like me at all?'

"That's not the point. Why don't you date a girl like Itota? She is not engaged yet."

'We are not talking about her. We are talking about you and me. Perhaps it is early to say so, but I think I'm falling in love with you.'

Evbu's heart began to thump. This was exactly how she had imagined a scene where a boy declared his love for her. Before she could say anything, Itota walked in. Her eyes lit up when she saw Jide.

'Hello, Jide,' she said, smiling.

'Hello! Look, Evbu, I must go now. Think over what I have just told you.'

'What has he just told you?' asked Itota when he had left.

'Oh, nothing!'

'I believe he is in love with you. I could sense it that first day.'

'Don't be silly, Itota. How can he be in love with me when he must have lots of glamorous girlfriends in Lagos?"

'Maybe he wants someone to keep him happy while he is here."

'That's not very flattering! Well, that person won't be me. Why don't you take him up?"

'Me? He doesn't even know that I exist. He just looks through me."

'That's your imagination at work. He asked for you as soon as he got in here.'

'I don't believe that."

Just then, Osaretin walked in.

'Hello, girls! Who was the boy I saw walking away from here just now?'

The girls looked at each other.

"That was Jide, Henry Idehen's guest from Lagos,' said Evbu.

'What did he want?'

'He came in to buy something,' snapped Itota. She, too, was beginning to feel that Osaretin was a shade too possessive.

'Oh, well, beware of these Lagos boys, Evbu. They are out for one thing only from girls.'

'I'm sure we can protect ourselves,' said Itota. Don't you think so, Evbu?'

'I do. Besides, he did not mean any harm by coming in here to do his shopping."

'Don't get me wrong, Evbu. It's just that I don't want any scandal. You're to be my wife and I care what you do and how you comport yourself. It's five o'clock now. Shall we go?'

'Yes, just a minute. Itota, let's add up the day's takings. I'll take it to my uncle's later."

Jide took to calling at the shop every day on one pretext or the other, and as time went on he did not bother to conceal the fact that he was in love with Evbu. At first, Evbu was scared incase he called while Osaretin was in the shop and there was a scene between the two. She was also worried about what Itota thought of her relationship with Jide. But she needn't have bothered. Itota understood perfectly well that they were in love with each other. At first she had striven to be noticed by Jide, but when he had mentioned casually on one of his visits to the shop that he was twenty, she had lost interest.

He was just the same age as her immediate younger brother. Evbu was the right age for him-eighteen. Now, if only Osaretin, whom she was secretly fond of, would pay a little attention to her...

Jide was very pleased to discover that he and Evbu had many things in common-a love for books, romantic and western films, poems, pop music and long walks. He told her a lot about himself. He was from Abeokuta in the Western Region, and the eldest of fourteen children. As heir to his father, who was a local chief and had several wives, much was expected of him. He intended studying to become a doctor on the completion of his course at King's College. He talked to Evbu about his life in Lagos, to which she listened avidly. She knew that Jide exaggerated for fun, but she did not mind. She just loved being with him and listening to him. Jide frequently brought Evbu little inexpensive gifts-earrings, rings and scarves. Then, one day, he gave her a bracelet with the inscription 'I LOVE YOU'.

'I really mean what is written on it," he said. 'Oh, come off it, Jide,' she laughed. 'What about all your girlfriends in Lagos?'

"They mean nothing to me,' he said, shrugging. "They have other boyfriends as well. At the moment you mean more to me than they do.'

'Let's not get carried away. I have a fiancé.' 'Yes, but do you really want to spend all your life with that man? He is too old for you. When he is forty you will just be twenty-three or so. Admit it! You don't really care for him. If you did, you would not let me see you.'

'You do have a nerve! So then, what are your plans? Are you going to marry me?' she teased.

'What about it? We could have a really nice time together in Lagos while you wait for me to qualify. You could share a room with Edith, my friend Chuks' girlfriend. She attends a Secretarial School. You may even decide to further your education while you wait for me.'

Evbu was attracted and fascinated by the thought of going to live in Lagos and seeing the bright lights! To actually go to school in Lagos and be called a Lagos girl like Ehi! That would be nice, but what about Osaretin? What about her family? It would break her mother's heart if she ran away, and she loved her family very much. Her father would surely kill her. What if Jide decided not to marry her afterwards? What would she do then? She would never be able to come back to Benin City to face all the mockery and false sympathy.

On the other hand, she might really be able to further her education and get a good job afterwards, and then marry Jide. They would both come to Benin to ask for her father's forgiveness. He would be so proud of her progress in life that he would forgive all. In her mind's eye she could see the fantastic house she would build for her parents. With Jide by her side forever, what more would she want in life then? Everything would just be great, or maybe not...

Meanwhile she continued to go home with Osaretin although her thoughts were full of Jide. She was grateful to Itota for her discretion in the whole affair. Whenever Jide was at the shop, she left them together and stayed close to the entrance where she could attend to customers. Evbu noticed that Itota was becoming sweet on Osaretin. She fussed over him when he came to take Evbu home, and flattered him about his way of dressing. Like all men, Osaretin was vain, and Itota's flattery pleased him. He paid her compliments in return. Evbu remarked on this to Jide.

'Don't you know her game?' asked Jide.

'Her game?' asked Evbu a bit foolishly. 'I thought she was just trying to divert Osaretin's attention from us.'

'Goodness! She wants Osaretin for herself, Evbu. I know her kind.'

Evbu was aghast. She certainly did not want any scandal. She comforted herself with the thought that everything would be alright as soon as Jide left. She was quite sure that she would never hear from him again.

The end of the relationship would break her heart but then what else did she expect? She would get married to Osaretin and settle down to have children like some of her mates. She would always cherish the memory of her brief relationship with Jide. He had opened up a new world for her. He did all the romantic things she had read about in novels, like helping her into taxis or reading out love poems to her. Osaretin never did any of those things. She did not dare let him see the lovely pop magazines that Jide bought for her from a departmental store. She was quite sure that he would laugh at her romantic ideas. Perhaps he was really too old for her. He was considerate though. He had looked after her father very well when he was ill and already her brothers had profited from the help he gave them in their studies. She really should be grateful to him for the interest he had taken in her family.

The eve of Jide's departure for Lagos was particularly painful for Evbu. He had come in as usual at midday and they had gone to their favourite 'buka for lunch. When they got back to the shop they chatted about nothing in particular. Then, suddenly, he drew her close and kissed her on the lips. It was her very first kiss and it was as lovely as she had imagined it would be.

'I will miss you, Evbu darling, 'he whispered. 'I don't believe you,' she tried to laugh. 'I bet you will not even remember to write to me after you have reunited with your Boss, Tinus and whatnots.'

'Maybe,' he teased. 'But don't forget what we discussed. It would be nice to have you with me in Lagos. Say, can I break the rule and come to see you at home this evening to say "goodbye"?"

'No, please Jide. There will be a scene if my father knows that I have been seeing another boy. My mother and brothers know about us though. I never hide anything from them."

'Will you tell them about our kiss this afternoon?' 'Perhaps. Please go now, Jide. Osaretin will be here any minute now, and you know he hates seeing you here. Have a nice journey back to Lagos. I might reply if you wrote before my wedding in June.'

'Don't mention your wedding to me. To think that you will soon belong to that old man. I can't see what you fancy in him. Anyway, we shall see.'

'Goodbye, Jide.'

'Goodbye. Take good care of yourself. Goodbye, Itota,' he said, raising his voice a little, 'and good luck in your manoeuvres.'

'What do you mean by that?' asked Itota, but he was already out of the shop.

'He was only teasing you,' said Evbu. 'Yes, but about what? There must have been something behind that remark of his.'

'Don't worry about it. You know that he jokes most of the time.'

"True. So, what are you going to do now that the "blue-eyed boy" is gone? You will miss him a lot, won't you?'

'Why should I? There was nothing in our relation- ship. We just enjoyed each other's company, and that was all.'

'One of my jokes, Evbu. I was not insinuating anything. You are eighteen and old enough to know your own mind.' That evening, Evbu moped about the house. Her brothers knew that Jide was leaving the following morning and they heaved a sigh of relief. Although they had met Jide several times at the shop and had liked and admired him, they felt that he was not ideal for their sister.

A relationship between him and Evbu could only bring trouble. They secretly sympathised with her, but at the same time they realised that Osaretin would make a very reliable husband. Anyway, Jide was going for good, and that would be the end of the whole affair. Even if he chose to come back during the next holiday, Evbu would be safely married and might no longer find him attractive. These things passed more quickly than people realised.

True to his word, Jide wrote every week-passion- ate letters full of his love for her and his desire to have her in Lagos. He had even contacted Edith, the girlfriend of his friend Chuks, who was willing to share her room with Evbu for ten naira a month. Although Evbu looked forward to these letters, which came through her brother Nosawaru, she decided not to reply to any of them so as not to en- courage him. Then, two weeks before her wedding, she wrote him a very ordinary letter beginning with: 'Dear Jide, ... In it, she told him about the preparations being made for her forthcoming wedding, and how far she had gone with the things she had bought for her trousseau. She did not need to write to him really about all these, but she felt that that was the only way she could show him that she had received all his letters.

When Jide got the letter, he smiled to himself. He had wondered why there had been no word from her. Although she had not exactly promised to reply to his letters, he knew that she was sufficiently fond of him not to be indifferent to his correspondence. He understood, of course, that Evbu would not want to write passionately to him while engaged to another man. She was very cautious in their relationship and Jide had the feeling that she was always applying a brake to her emotions.

Apart from his fierce determination to get on in life and become a successful doctor, his immediate burning desire was to bring Evbu to Lagos and have her to himself. It would be nice to show off a non-Lagos girl to his friends. He was used to being adored by girls, but the fact that Evbu had never treated him as if he were a 'super- human being' did not bother him. He could not quite define his feelings as regards Evbu. He knew that he had never wanted any other girl so much as he wanted her.

Maybe the attraction was because she belonged to someone else, but he was not quite sure. Marriage with Evbu would be out of the question though, because his father had always impressed on him that he must choose his bride from Abeokuta. Apart from that, he considered Evbu's standard of education much too low for him. But of course he was not going to tell her that.

The next letter he wrote was even more passionate than all the others, saying how much he loved Evbu and how his mind was wandering from his studies because of his constant thoughts of her. He did not ask her not to go through with her wedding for that might make her more determined than ever to do so and he did not want such a thing on his conscience. The decision was to be hers.

Evbu ran away three days before her wedding. Some days before she had hastily gathered together her best clothes, put them in a bag and had hidden the bag in the shop. She had told nobody of her intention. The thought of the oncoming wedding was too much for her and she knew that she did not really want to spend the rest of her life with Osaretin. She would go to Lagos, get a job and send back Osaretin's bride price. She would even send more than he had paid if she could, so as to cover the cost of whatever he had bought for her.

That morning she left for work as usual. She had with her some money she had been able to save, and all the letters Jide had written to her. Evbu felt very nervous but tried hard to conceal it.

At about 8.15 she told Itota she was hungry and wanted to buy some akara balls round the corner. She went down to the store at the back of the shop, retrieved her bag and walked quickly to the Motor Park to take a taxi to Lagos. She was just in time to take the nine o'clock '404'. While waiting for the car to move she scribbled a note to her brother Nosa telling him what she had done and giving Edith as her contact address. She begged him to reassure her mother of her safety, and promised to write when things were better. Then she bought a magazine to cover her face with while the car went through the town.

Chapter 3

The journey was uncomfortable and uneventful. The car carried seven passengers, including a baby, instead of five. It was hot and the baby kept screaming. When they stopped for the passengers to eat, Evbu did not leave the car for fear of being seen by people she knew.

When they got to Lagos it was raining, but Evbu's first view of the city was an exciting one. Modern buildings lined the streets where people and cars swarmed in huge numbers. There was street trading on a large scale. When they got to Yaba roundabout she saw the College of Technology that her brothers had talked so much about. Further on, she saw a sign showing the way to the University of Lagos.

There were shops everywhere and they seemed to be full of things to buy. No wonder people talked so much about Lagos. Just walking about here would make her happy. The only thing she did not like was the filth. There were heaps of garbage on the road- side and dustbins were overflowing. She saw one or two beggars rummaging about amongst the debris and shuddered.

Before the driver of her taxi stopped at Oyingbo, she could hear shouts of 'Oyingbo bo le', 'Oyingbo bo le', 'Oyingbo come down', from the conductors of buses at the bus stop. There were swarms of people everywhere, despite the rain, and music was blaring from record shops. The taxi stopped and she got out. The driver lifted her bag down from the rack.

'When are you going back to Benin?' he asked. 'On Friday morning,' she replied. 'Okay, make sure you wait for my car. You see, I'm a careful driver. Ten years on the Lagos/Benin road and no accident,' he said proudly.

'That's very good,' laughed Evbu. 'I shall wait for you when I get to the Park on Friday."

She walked over to a stall in the market and asked a young girl in school uniform the way to Denton Street. Surprisingly, it was not far at all and very shortly she was at Edith's house. She was told that Edith's room was the first on the ground floor, close to the gate. No one was sure whether she was in or not as they had not seen her that day. Evbu knocked on the door and, after some time, a girl came to the door. She was about twenty-four, of average height and light in complexion. She wore a housecoat and the previous night's make-up.

'Good afternoon, I am Evbu Isibor from Benin City. I am, er, I believe Jide Jones has, er, spoken to you about me. I, er, have...'

'Of course, you're Evbu,' said Edith, helping the poor nervous girl. 'Jide has spoken many times about you to Chuks, my boyfriend, and me. He told me you might come to Lagos and that he would like me to share my room with you, but he did not tell me exactly when you would be coming. So, you're welcome! Is this your first visit to Lagos!"

'Yes,' said Evbu, a little bit ashamed to sound provincial.

'Well, never mind. There is always a first time in everything. Come in, please. Don't pay any attention to the state of the room. Everything is upside down. Dump your things in that corner."

"Thank you,' said Evbu gratefully. She had been a bit apprehensive about turning up without notice on a stranger's doorstep, but Edith seemed a friendly soul. 'So, you're Evbu! I must say you are even prettier than Jide told us! Since he came back from his holiday in Benin he is always talking about you. He's quite crazy about you. He calls you his "queen"."

Evbu blushed. She warmed up to this girl who was so nice and flattering. She needed someone to take her in hand in Lagos.

'I'm sorry that I can't offer you something to eat. My pot is empty and I haven't had the strength to go to the market, but there is an excellent 'buka' nearby. You will find that many people in this area eat or buy their cooked food from 'bukas'. They are such a help. No messy cooking. I don't hate cooking,' she added hastily, 'I just can't find the time for it. My studies, you know.'

'I'll do our cooking, then. I adore cooking.

'Oh, would you? That would be nice. I'm out most of the time, though. I go to my boyfriend

51

most even- ings and sometimes I spend the night there. We shall get engaged once he can afford my bride price.

"That's nice! Will the wedding be in Lagos?' 'Oh, no! It has to be at home so that all my people can attend.'

That evening, Chuks, Edith's boyfriend, called to take her out, and was introduced to Evbu. 'So! This is Jide's "queen"! Nice to meet you.. Does "Double J" know of your arrival? He has told us a lot about you.'

'No, he doesn't know I'm in town. I...I just decided to come and there was no time to alert him. Please do you know how I can reach him?'

'I shall tell him you're in town on my way home this evening. I don't think you are likely to see him before Sunday though. He is very serious about his studies and rarely takes special permission to go out."

When Edith and Chuks had gone out, Evbu locked the door carefully using all the bolts and then went behind the partition into the 'bedroom' to undress. The place was in a mess. Clothes everywhere! Edith might be pretty and sophisticated, but she was certainly untidy! Evbu tidied up the place, folding up some dresses and hanging up others. She was glad to have something to do to take her mind off her problems. When she finished tidying up, she made the bed.

Later on she went to one of the three bath- rooms shared by all the tenants and had a shower. She was a bit shy going past all the other rooms on the ground floor, with the occupants either cooking or relaxing outside, to get to the bathroom. She had never seen so many people living in one house. To her it seemed like a small village. She was very tired that night and slept deeply.

Edith came home at about seven the next morning, dressed up and went out again saying that she was going to school. Evbu discovered later on that that was the pattern of Edith's life. Sometimes she would go out for a short while during the day and spend the rest of the day in. Sometimes she disappeared for a day or two. Evbu decided right from the onset that she would have to cook.

Buying food three times a day from the 'buka' seemed costly to her and the place was not terribly hygienic. So the next day she went down to Oyingbo market to buy food. She got by with sign language and Pidgin English, but she found everything expensive. How did people survive in a place like this? She would have to get a job as quickly as she could.

She was disappointed when she learned from Edith that, though extremely happy to know that Evbu had arrived, Jide could not come to see her before Sunday. Two whole days more to go. Well, she could go sightseeing around the area. That Saturday, Edith stayed in throughout the day to do her laundry. She had so much to wash that Evbu had to ask her how she managed to get such fabulous dresses on a student's allowance.

'My father is a doctor in Aba, you know. Very rich. He has a private hospital, and several doctors work for him. He was very disappointed when I did not want to train as a doctor. All that blood and broken bones, ugh!

Evbu looked at her enviously but wondered why a doctor's daughter attended a Commercial School in- stead of a Grammar School, and lived in such a poor room. Apart from that at twenty-three or twenty- four Edith ought to be in a much higher institution of learning, money being no problem.

At last it was Sunday and Evbu was terribly ex- cited at the thought of seeing Jide again. She got up early, so as to use the bathroom before the rush, and then dressed with care. Although she had very few dresses, she had good dress sense. Edith had complimented her once on her choice of material and style. It did not show too much that she had only just arrived from the provinces. Given the money, she knew that she could dress with even more sophistication than Edith.

Edith got up early too, got dressed and said that she was going to spend the day with Chuks. Evbu was grateful. She knew that Edith was tactfully leaving the coast clear for Jide and herself. She vow- ed that she would do all in her power to show appreciation for Edith's kindness. Not every girl would willingly share her room with a stranger.

Jide came at about 10.00 a.m. As soon as he entered the room she ran to him and was gathered up in his arms. They kissed and then both began to talk at once. Jide wanted to know what had happened to change Evbu's plans, and she narrated everything. He was not pleased to hear that she had been going about sightseeing.

'You should lie low for some weeks, you know. Benin City is not that far from Lagos.'

"They can't come and take me back by force to Benin. After all, I'm eighteen.'

'Yes, but all the same, they could declare you missing. You don't want your photograph appearing in the papers saying that you've run away from home, do you?'

'No, I don't. That was why I sent a note to my brother Nosawaru. My mother will not let Papa do anything drastic. Since she knows that I'm safe, she will not worry too much. My brothers should write soon, anyway. The pressing problem is that I must get a job fast. The little money I have will not go far. I must try to pay my way.'

'No, it won't. Especially in a place like Lagos. You're lucky you live near Oyingbo market. Things are a bit cheaper there than on the Lagos Island Look, to help out, I will pay your share of the rent. I know that is not much, but I'm afraid that's all I can afford out of my monthly allowance. If I have anything extra I will help out with money for food too.'

"Thanks Jide. I'm sure I'll get a job soon so that I can save enough money for College.'

"That's a good idea. You could even work during the day, and attend an evening school. Can't your brothers help?'

'No, they can't. They too want to study further and they are saving up for this, and paying for overseas tuition as well.'

"That's good, you know. I like ambitious people." They played the records which Jide had brought with him and they danced. Later, she prepared lunch and she and Jide ate.

'Hm! This is nice,' said Jide. 'So my "queen" cooks well?'

'I have to. My father is very fussy about his food. He refuses to eat anything that does not taste nice. Poor Ma will have to cope with it all now.'

'Well, you can't cook for your father forever. You will have to have your own home.'

The inevitable happened that afternoon and Evbu was glad that it was with Jide. It was painful but tender, and they both felt very much in love. At four, Jide reluctantly left to catch his bus. He left several books and magazines for her to read to pass the time. He said that it might not be possible for him to visit every Sunday as he was preparing for his final examinations in October but he would write.

The weeks fled past and so did Evbu's money, although her brothers sent her a little extra. She was touched by their kindness. In their letter they told of how their mother had fainted when she heard that Evbu had run away, and how their father vowed that he would never allow her to set foot in that house again. However, things were almost back to normal at the time of writing.

They had explained to their mother that Evbu had not been keen on get- ting married so young, and would have preferred to go for further studies if the money had been available, but had lacked the courage to explain things to their parents. Their mother had accepted this but had said that Evbu should be told not to do anything silly, and to avoid the temptations of a big city which they had heard so much about. Moreover, she was to write home regularly so that they would know that she was alright. After the first day their father had refused to say anything more about her. Meanwhile the brothers had refunded the bride price to Osaretin so that he would not use 'juju' on her. Some weeks later, Osaretin was seen with Itota at a wake-keeping ceremony.

For Evbu, things were not at all easy. For admission into a school for nurses a candidate had to have at least a Class 4 certificate. She did not fancy teaching, so she decided to try Commercial Colleges. She got admission into several, but when Jide checked at the Ministry of Education it was discovered that these schools were not approved. This meant that at the end of the course, one could not get a good job with the certificate issued. After much delay, she got admission into an approved college which offered both basic and commercial subjects.

At first Evbu was very pleased with her success, but she soon began to fret about the fees. They were not much, but then she had no job. Jide could not help and she could not possibly encroach on her brothers' charity again. Borrowing from Edith was out of the question for where would she get the money to pay back? If only she could get the first term's fees. Or even the deposit of thirty naira so that the place could be reserved for her! Already she had received two letters from the School saying that if she did not pay up by a certain date the place would be given to someone else. Her increasing anxiety soon affected her health and Edith became concerned by the condition of the girl who had come to be almost a younger sister to her.

'Evbu,' said Edith one morning, 'what's the matter with you? Are you ill? You spend most of the time in bed. When you are out of it you just sit around. Is there anything wrong?'

'I'm not feeling very well. I can't sleep at night and I can hardly eat.'

'No wonder you look like a scarecrow. I'm sorry I did not notice earlier. I have been so wrapped up in my own problems. Have you seen the doctor? You're protected aren't you? So, it can't be a baby. Is it Jide? I have not seen him around here for some time. Are you quarrelling?'

'No. Jide's alright. He's preparing hard for his A levels, and so cannot come very often,'

'Yes, he is very serious with his books. Why don't you see the doctor? You might have malaria.'

'I don't think I'm all that sick, Edith. It's just that I have a big problem. I see no way out!'

'My goodness!' said Edith, alarmed. 'Whatever can be the matter? You sound really desperate. I've never known you to be like that. Tell me about it. It might not be as bad as you think.'

"It's about my admission to that College."

'Oh, is that all? If they have cancelled your place, you can always apply elsewhere. We might even use long legs to get you in. I know someone who...'

'No, my place still holds, but I haven't got the money to pay the fees. I don't even have the money to pay the deposit. A letter came some days ago saying that if I don't pay up by Friday, that's in two days, my place will be offered to someone else. I have no money, no prospects of a job, and no one to help.'

'Why don't you send a message home for help?'

'My people are poor and they cannot help. Jide cannot help either. Oh, I wish I had stayed in Benin and got married to Osaretin. I would not have landed myself in the mess I am in now. Maybe this is God's way of telling me that what I did was wrong. In a big place like Lagos, one would think that jobs would be easy to come by. I just don't know what to do. I desperately want to further my education. I have always wanted to. That was one of the reasons I came to Lagos!'

She broke down and began to weep. Before long she had told Edith all about how

she ran away from home and came to Lagos.
Edith was sympathetic.

'I'm sorry to know that you are so hard up,
Evbu.

I like you and I wish I could lend you the
money, but I'm saving hard for a purpose. You
see, Chuks and I will be leaving for Britain next
June for further studies. We've been saving hard
for the past two years. Now we have got
admission and will be paying our fees shortly.
Chuks will do banking and I will do catering.
First, we shall go home and get married in
April.'

'Aren't you lucky? But what about your
secretarial course? How are you able to save on
your allowance, or is your father sponsoring
you?'

'Oh, that,' laughed Edith. 'Listen! I will come
clean with you. I don't study. I am a hostess-in

short, I'm a good-time girl. That shocks you, doesn't it?'

'What?' cried Evbu, stupefied. 'You don't look like one. I mean, I mean, you look quite decent and all that. You speak good English, too.'

Edith shrugged. 'I think you're thinking of the good-time girls in the provinces. This is the capital, and girls who do my type of work come from all walks of life-rich and poor, illiterate and educated. I really am what I've told you. Chuks does not know the whole truth, though. He thinks that I'm a hostess in the club's casino, which is what I told him.'

'Won't he find out about what you are actually doing at present?'

'No way. I go with expatriates only, and I am very discreet about it."

'Do you go to the same nightclub?" 'Not always."

'Aren't you afraid you might catch something? My mother said that girls who sleep around catch diseases. I would be afraid."

'I have a very good doctor and, luckily, I have never caught anything. A girl who has only one boyfriend can also catch diseases.'

'Hm! It's very courageous of you, anyway. I wish I had half your courage.'

'Oh, I will try anything once.'

'Well, you know best what suits you. My problem is still a long way from being solved.'

'I was coming to that. Why don't you come to the nightclub with me?'

"To date men? Never! I would almost die from shame. What would Jide say when he hears about it'? What would my parents say?'

'Why should Jide ever know? We won't go to clubs on the Island or around here. There are many different clubs. I don't attach myself to any in particular.'

'Hm! Even then!"

'Look, as soon as you've made enough money for your studies, you could call it quits. In this area here I'm known as a student. No client ever calls here. 1 would not have told you anything about it but for the fact that I have come to look upon you as a sister. Also, I know how very discreet and loyal you are.'

'Will I be able to hide my activities from Jide?"
"That's your affair. How old are you now? Nineteen? Well, you're old enough to know what you want to do. The other thing would be for you to get a sugar daddy to sponsor you, but I doubt if you would be able to cope with wives and girlfriends coming to scratch out your eyes.

'But don't you feel humiliated when you have to sit down waiting for someone to approach you?'
'Why should I? I pay to go in like other people. What I do is my own affair. Anyway, I'm not trying to make up your mind for you. I only made a suggestion. If you have some other way of solving your little problem, you can go ahead."

'Unfortunately, I don't. Please don't be cross with me Edith. I was not trying to criticise your way of living, it's just that I have never looked at life that way. Can I come with you today? I can always back out if I don't fancy it, can't I?'

'Sure! Don't do anything you don't want to do.'

Chapter 4

So Evbu, against all she had been taught, went out with Edith that evening. She felt very self-conscious in one of Edith's long evening dresses. Both girls made up carefully. Evbu was surprised to find that no one stared at them. They took a bus to a club in Apapa. When they got there Edith insisted that they should go to the 'Ladies' to freshen up. There they found many other girls who eyed them as soon as they got in, and Evbu felt nervous. Edith greeted some of them and pointedly ignored others. She gave Evbu a cigarette, and lit one for herself.

'What for?' asked Evbu in a low voice.
'You should smoke to put you in a good mood. I never smoke myself unless I am in a nightclub.

Drag on it slowly, then release the smoke gradually.'

Evbu did as she was told and choked. When she stopped coughing and tried again it was not so bad. The cigarette made her lightheaded, and she did not dread the thought of what lay ahead that night so much. Before they went into the club, Edith gave her some advice. She should not take alcohol and, if she did not fancy someone who came to her, she should politely refuse his offer of drinks. When she (Edith) shook her head while looking Evbu in the eyes, she should know that the man with her was no good.

Evbu looked round. The club was rapidly filling up and the place was becoming stuffy and thick with smoke. People kept streaming in- couples, single girls, single men-all colours. The single girls bought drinks, sat down and waited. From time to time a girl would get up and go and repair her make- up. As they passed between the tables, they swung their hips provocatively. Some of them had their bottoms pinched by the men. Evbu shuddered when she noticed that, and when Edith suggested they go to the 'Ladies' she declined.

The evening progressed. Several men had come to sit at their table but Edith gave them no encouragement. Evbu was secretly glad. Although she was desperately in need of money, she was hoping inside her that the mission would be a failure and she would not get herself into that kind of trade. Her only consolation was that Jide never came to town on weekdays. She had earlier decided that she would operate, if she had to, only on weekdays. She just hoped that she would not let anything slip out when she was with Jide. By midnight, they had rejected all the men who had come to them.

'Evbu, come on,' said Edith, 'let's go to another club. There doesn't seem to be such action here tonight.'

'Is it far? My feet are killing me. These shoes are a bit on the small side.'

'Sorry about that. It is just around the corner." Things were certainly livelier at the second club. There was more space and the atmosphere was gay.

All the seats had been taken up and they had to bribe a waiter to squeeze them in somewhere. They ordered cokes, and Edith urged her to try another cigarette. The music was good and very shortly, the girls were led to the dance floor. Evbu noticed that some single men and girls were dancing by themselves. When the band stopped, Evbu's escort took her back to her seat and went and brought over his drink. He called a waiter and wanted to buy the girls a drink, but Edith told him in a cold voice not to bother. Evbu was surprised.

The man was Lebanese, tall and good-looking, and seemed to have the cash to spend, judging by his appearance. Discouraged by Edith's attitude, the man soon left for another girl.

'What was the matter, Edith? I thought the man looked a good sort.'

'He probably is, but you will have trouble getting your money from him. I dated him once and regretted it. He is no gentleman at all. He could not recognise me in the dim light."

'Good riddance, then.'

After this, the girls danced a lot with different men. Then two Europeans came and sat at their table after asking their permission to do so. Evbu could see that Edith liked them right from the start, probably because of their polite manners.

Very shortly an introduction was made and they chatted and then danced. The men bought them drinks and cigarettes. By the time the floor show came on, at 2 a.m., the girls had agreed to go with them. Edith did most of the talking and bargaining. Evbu was too nervous to talk, and to be quite frank she did not understand half of what the men were saying. They seemed to talk in their throats. Edith later explained everything to her in a low voice. The men were staying at a nearby hotel and they wanted their forty naira each. Evbu confessed to her that she was company for the night. They were willing to pay then everything was fine.

Edith told her not to be ill at ease but, if Edith felt that the men were okay. Immediately after the floor show, all four left for the hotel.

The girls got back home next morning at 8.30 and went straight to bed. When she got up at midday, Evbu tidied the flat and made lunch. Although she felt ashamed of the previous night she was in a strangely exhilarated mood. She was now in a position to pay the deposit for a place at the Commercial College.

It was as if she was in a dream. Twenty-four hours ago her case had seemed a hopeless one; now she was in the pink. On the way home in a taxi, she had told Edith that she felt that she was cheating on Jide. Edith laughed at her and said that she would probably commit suicide if she knew half what Jide was up to and that, since she was not married to him, what exactly was she afraid of?

Later that afternoon Evbu went to pay the deposit at the College. She was quite thrilled. She had wanted to pay part of the school fees with the balance but Edith told her to hold on to it. She might need it for books or school uniforms.

'But aren't we going to the club tonight? I could make some more money."

'Easy, girl,' laughed Edith. 'Business does not come good every evening. Sometimes, you draw a blank. You don't regard what you were given as your profit for the night; you have to deduct the gate fee you paid, the drinks you bought and the taxi fare. Then you invest whatever is left for the next outing. This time you might be lucky and get some more money but you might be unlucky and lose what you have invested.'

'How?', 'For one, you may not get the type of client you like; for another, you might not be paid what was promised. So you see, you have to part with what you have only if you can afford to. You have to eat as well. Yesterday, I paid for everything, but today you will have to take care of yourself financially even though we shall be together.'

'You are a very sensible lady, Edith. What would I do without you? I'm sure I shall get myself into all sorts of trouble when you leave for abroad. I'm so naive.'

'Never mind. You're still very young. This is the time for you to learn, though. By the way, how are you going to explain your sudden affluence to Jide?' 'I shall tell him that you loaned me the money for my school fees.'

'No, that won't do. He does not know anything about my private life, so how will you explain the source of this money I am able to lend you? I think the best thing is for you to say that your brothers sent you some money from home. As for new clothes, you could always tell him that you got them from me.'

'Alright, thank you, Edith."

When Jide visited her at the end of her first week he noticed a difference in her-she seemed more confident of herself. He was pleased to know that she would be going to the Commercial College after all.

Now that he earned some money, Jide was able to take Evbu round Lagos, showing her all the places of interest. Evbu enjoyed all these visits, not only because of their novelty, but because she and Jide were together. Sometimes they went to the pictures but Jide said they could not go to the nightclubs because he always had to be in early. Just as well, though Evbu. She was not at all anxious to go to nightclubs with him-not while she was still operating anyway.

Edith regretted that Evbu could not work at weekends for she assured her that that was when real money was made. Evbu, however, stuck to her decision. She knew that she would need the weekends to catch up on her studies now she had started school.

Soon it was April. Edith and Chuks left to get married in their home town and Evbu was on her own. She missed Edith badly and was a bit scared to go to the clubs on her own but, as she needed to make money, she had to. It was not as difficult as she had expected. She had made a few acquaintances among the girls and so she had people to chat with.

She had written home to her parents and brothers that she had a part-time job and had begun school. Her mother and brothers wrote back to congratulate her, but she had a constant pang of pain that her father had still not forgiven her and would not communicate with her. She wrote to her brothers about it but they told her not to worry, that their father was as proud of her as ever but pretended that he was still hurt by her going away. They had over-heard him telling one of his friends, who had asked after Evbu, that she was in a College in Lagos training to be a secretary.

Idemudia in his letter said that it would be a great help if she could send some money home: their father was going to retire shortly and his monthly pension was going to be very small and he was still trying to educate the rest of his children. Ebvu was touched when she read all this. She knew what it was for money to be short in the house. Her poor mother would be working her fingers to the bone thinking of ways to economise and at the same time please her family. So, the next day, she went to the bank and got out N60. This she sent to her mother through Idemudia and from then on sent regular amounts.

When Chuks and Edith returned to Lagos and were waiting for their visas to be issued, Jide gained admission to the Medical School. He was wild with joy and took Evbu out for a celebration. At first he wanted to take her to a nightclub but she hastily declined saying that she would rather have a drink and then go and watch a late night movie. He was surprised because when she first came to Lagos she had always expressed her wish to be taken to nightclubs.

'I thought that I would give you a treat tonight to celebrate my admission. Why the change of attitude?'

'It's just that I would rather we went to a less crowded place where I could have you to myself."

'Don't you want to dance?'

'Not particularly. I have a slight headache, and don't want to make it worse' she lied.

'Would you rather we had a stroll along the Marina, then came back here and stayed in? I am happy to do anything."

'Oh, no. The headache is not as bad as that. Let's go for a drink and then to the pictures.'

'Good idea!'

They went to the 'Chic Restaurant', had some snacks and drank to his success. 'And here is to the future Dr Jide Jones,' he said, raising his glass.

'Cheers!' she said, raising hers.

'Just imagine it! A few years from now, I shall be a qualified doctor and when I have enough money, I will set up my own practice. Gosh, I will make pots of money, travel and see the world."

'What about me? Don't I come in, in your future plans? Will I become Mrs Jide Jones?' she teased. 'I don't see why not. That's all a long way off, anyway. I have sent a telegram to my parents telling them the good news. They will be so proud of me. My mother will travel to her village nearby to tell her parents. I bet she will tell them that I'm already a doctor, so when next I go to see granny I expect she will complain non-stop about her ailments-real or imaginary."

'Really,' laughed Evbu, 'that's nice! Your granny will be your very first patient then."

'And what a patient!'

'Hello, Double J, old boy! Nice to see your face again,' said a tall young man who stood up behind Jide and placed his hands lightly over his eyes to prevent him turning around, and then he winked at Evbu.

'Who is it?' said Jide, trying to turn around.

'Guess!'

Tunde! Sambo! Femi! Onyebuchi!'

'No! No! No! No!'

'Well, who is it then?'

'Ask your friend to describe me.'

'Evbu, who is it! Describe him.'

'I have never seen him before,' began Evbu nervously, 'but he is tall, er, er....'

'Let me see,' said Jide, wrestling his hands from his eyes, and turning around.

'Steve Mayo!' he shouted, causing people who were dining to look his way. 'Wherever did you spring from? I thought your family had left Lagos."

'Yes, we had."

'What about your brother?'

'He is here on a visit, same as I am. He's outside the restaurant. I came back to collect the keys I had left on our table, and I was just going back to join him when I caught sight of your companion and then of you-in that order.'

'I believe you,' laughed Jide. 'I'm sure it happened in that order.'

'You bet. Say, come on out and say "hello" to Jamie. I'm sure he will be glad to see you again. Excuse us, lady.'

'A few minutes please, Evbu,' said Jide as they both moved off.

When he returned to the table he found her looking bored and staring into her drink.

'I'm terribly sorry, darling,' he said as he sat down.

'I thought you were never coming back.' 'You know how it is when you meet old schoolmates.

You chat and chat and ask after this and that. If we are to go to the pictures, come on, let's get started.'

The film was a lousy one, but they hardly paid any attention anyway as they were busy telling each other all that had happened since they last met.

For weeks after Edith and Chuks had left Lagos, Evbu avoided clubs. When she ran short of money she had to begin again.

It was on her first night back that she ran into Mr Jackson, an Australian businessman based in London. She had refused several prospective clients that night and was wondering if she should not call it a day and go home, when he joined her. He was a tall, handsome and athletic-looking man. She had caught him staring at her as she sat apart from the other girls, refusing clients.

To Pete Jackson, Evbu was the best girl in the room. 'Oho! an African queen,' he had said to himself as soon as he saw her. Her tall and elegant appearance appealed to him. She seemed somehow out of place there. She seemed more like one of those much sought-after hostesses who graced great social events. His experienced eyes took in her clothes at a glance-cheap but tasteful, he decided. Those clothes probably cost a fortune here. It would be fun to be able to buy her really great clothes. She had the figure to carry off anything.

Pete caught sight of Evbu drinking and gathering up her things, and in another second he found himself in the seat at her table. On reflecting later on, he could not explain the impulse that had driven him. He just knew that he had a desperate urge not to let her walk away from his life.

'Hello,' he said as he sat down. 'I'm Pete Jackson. Can I buy you a drink? Please don't say "no".'

Yes, please,' she said and smiled. She was surprised to find him at her table as she was getting ready to leave the club, but she liked him on sight and did not mind much. She liked his pleasant manners. It was the beginning of a relationship they both came to enjoy very much.

Pete Jackson was twenty-eight and married, but lived apart from his wife and daughter. When Evbu told him of her love for Jide, and her hope that they would marry when they had both finished their education, he wished her luck, but it was obvious that his own experience had left him with little confidence that any marriage could be a success. Pete accepted Evbu's lifestyle without question. He recognised that all too often people have to do things quite alien to their natures in order to make things easier for themselves. In that respect he was as much of a realist as Edith, who had once said exactly the same thing to Evbu.

Evbu was happy. Pete's generosity meant that she no longer had to go to the clubs looking for clients and it was as if a great weight had been lifted from her. She was almost able to wipe out the memories of that part of her young life. Her only regret was that she could not share her elation with Jide.

When Jide was around at weekends Evbu was very careful not to let anything about Pete give her away. She never wore any of the new dresses he brought her, and she would exclaim delightedly over any little present that Jide gave her. Nothing changed in the relationship between them. They were still very much in love with each other.

But her school work began to suffer as a result of taking so much time off. The Principal called her and advised her to pay more attention to her studies. She took the advice lightly and at the end of that term she failed her examinations. She was full of remorse. She had been one of the best students in class and had had a very good record until then. Jide was quite sympathetic but told her off firmly. He could not understand, he said, why a perfectly brilliant student could suddenly start doing very badly. She must be moving with an idle gang, he suggested. Pete was sympathetic and added his encouragement to study hard, reminding her that she had only two terms to go before the end of her course.

He promised that if she did well in her RSA examinations, he would sponsor a trip to London for her. By the beginning of her last term Evbu had caught up again and was preparing for her RSA papers. At the same time Jide was busy preparing for his exams. He had just one more session to go before he qualified. He saw Evbu on alternate weekends now so as to give him more time to study. His love for her, he said, had not diminished but he just had to make a good grade. She did not mind much when he failed to turn up even on these alternate weekends, but she began to suspect that he must be seeing other girls too. She knew that he had girlfriends on the campus. What about all those girls who eyed her when she went with him to dances there? It would be silly to think that, living in such close proximity, he would not date any of them. She was almost twenty-three now and experienced enough to know that boys usually played around. The thought of her Jide with another girl made her heart ache but, thinking of her relationship with Pete, she felt she was in no position to complain. Time would take care of everything.

A few days after Evbu finished her examinations she received a telegram from home saying that her father was seriously ill and that he kept asking for her. She dropped Jide a line explaining things and then travelled to Benin City. It was her first trip home since she had run away on the eve of her wedding. She was impressed by the improvement that had taken place in the town. There were new buildings and roads, a bus service and lots of taxis.

When she got home, she was warmly received by all the members of her family. She was shocked to find how old and emaciated her father looked. He hugged her weakly but happily and there were tears in his eyes. She was told that he had collapsed while working in the garden at the back of the house. A doctor had been called in but there had been no improvement in his condition. She stayed by his sick bed most of the time and had her meals in his room. She asked him for forgiveness, and he murmured that there was nothing to forgive. If only she had told him that she did not care for Osaretin no one would have forced her to marry him. He had no regrets because she was now doing so well in Lagos. Perhaps that was the life God had planned for her. He prayed for her continued progress in life and told her to always bring honour to the name of the family. A few days later he died in his sleep.

When Evbu arrived back in Lagos she was surprised to find Jide waiting for her at the Motor Park. Then she remembered that school had begun about two weeks before and that he must have come back from Abeokuta where he had gone for the Christmas holiday.

'Happy New Year, darling,' said Jide, hugging and kissing her, to the amusement of some of the passers-by. 'I have been coming here for the past three days. I knew that you would try and come back this week because your results would be out soon. In fact they are out, your classmate Chinwe told me, and you passed very well."

Evbu jumped for joy when she heard this, and hugged Jide. She was pleased that Jide had taken the trouble to come and meet her. He was very considerate when he wanted to be. But the mood of relaxed understanding between them was quickly disturbed.

When she opened the door to her room, the new clothes that Pete had brought a few days before she left for Benin were still on the bed. She hastily tried to conceal them, but Jide had noticed them. He picked up one of them.

'Hm! This is a very expensive dress. Did you win the pools?' he asked.

'Oh, er, er, Edith sent them to me through an air hostess friend of hers."

'Really, that was very kind of her. For one mad moment I thought a sugar daddy had bought them for you.'

'Don't you trust me?'

'I suppose. But seriously speaking, I can't bear the thought of other men being close to you." When we first met in Benin you told me your girlfriends in Lagos meant nothing to you. Why are you bothered about whether I have another boy- friend or not? Don't you have other girls?'

"That's beside the point. The important thing is how I feel about you. You mean a lot to me. I just can't explain it.' It was true. He had dated more sophisticated and educated girls, but somehow he was always drawn back to Evbu.

'How did the Christmas holiday go?'
asked Evbu, hurriedly changing the subject. 'It
was dull. You were not with me so how did you
expect me to pass the time?' he said and winked
at her. 'I spent most of the time reading."

'I'm sure you did, bookworm.'

'When do you start looking for a job?'

'Right away, I guess. I don't have to wait
for the result of the RSA examinations which
will come out in about three or four months'
time. I can work with the certificate from my
college."

'So, the money should start rolling in
shortly?' 'Sure! There will be no shortage of it."
'Great! Then I don't need to study so hard. I will
just relax and live off you!"

Five months later, in June, Evbu still had
not found a job. She had not hunted seriously,

though. Pete came twice during this period and they were together most of the time that he was not working. Now that the strain of studies was removed. She was a relaxed and happy person. She was not living in luxury but she did not lack money. Pete saw to that. He did not give her money in cash anymore, but went directly to her bank where he would pay money into her account and then would casually refer to it later.

Early in June, she got the results of her RSA examinations-she made 100/50 in shorthand and typewriting and she passed well in the other commercial subjects she had taken. She was wild with joy and raced immediately to the campus to tell Jide. He told her to hang around till evening when they would both go out to celebrate.

The next day, she sent a cable to inform Pete of her success. Some days later, she got one informing her to call at the desk of a foreign airline in Lagos to collect a return ticket to London. This was beyond her wildest dreams. To go abroad! She had not actually thought that Pete would keep his promise, for he had said no more about it since the day he made it. The only problem was how to explain her absence to Jide.

He made this easy some days later when he said that he was going to Ibadan for the long vacation.

'Why?' asked Evbu. 'Don't you want to be with me here in Lagos?"

'Of course I do. But, you see, a cousin of mine promised me a job for the holiday and I don't want to miss the opportunity of earning some money."

'Can't you get a job here in Lagos?'

'So far, nothing. I don't want to waste my time hanging around doing nothing."

'Oh, I see. So I shall be all alone in Lagos for at least eight weeks."

'Cheer up, darling. I wish I could stay here with you. Hmm, that would be lovely," he added, kissing her.

As soon as Jide left for Ibadan, she began to process her travel papers. It was not quite as easy as she had thought but, at last, she succeeded in getting everything ready. Meanwhile Pete's letter came, explaining that he was afraid that he could only afford to sponsor Evbu in London for ten days, and that he hoped that she would not mind. Mind! Evbu was amused. Even three or four days were enough for her. She knew how expensive hotel lodgings could be in Nigeria, let alone in Europe. She wrote to Edith and Chuks informing them of her impending trip, then she wrote to Jide telling him that she was going to spend some weeks in the village with her grandmother.

She was met at Heathrow Airport by Pete, Chuks and Edith. She was very glad to see them all.

'Let's take a cab back to my place then you can talk about old times,' said Pete, smiling. 'Later, I'll take Evbu to her hotel.'

Although it was summer, Evbu felt terribly cold; otherwise she fell in love with London. She visited all the famous places and Pete was the perfect host. He could not take her everywhere, so he bought her a tourist guide and told her to get on with it. Every night they had dinner together and he listened attentively to how she had spent the day. Once, he even asked a girl in his office to take her out shopping.

Evbu noticed that no one cared about the colour of the people you were with. She knew of course that there must be colour prejudice somewhere, but on the surface everything was normal, barring some old people who hurriedly got up when she sat near them on the train or in the bus. She was amused by this. The people probably thought that their skin would become tinged with black if they came too close to her.

She spent the weekend with Edith and Chuks and was highly amused when they tried to match her off with several Nigerian boys. In her heart she knew that there would never really be anyone else for her except Jide, but she played along and went out with these boys.

When Evbu got back to Lagos, she travelled immediately to Benin City to see her family. Her mother had recovered from the shock of her husband's death and her sisters and brothers were doing fairly well. She had brought presents for everyone and they were excited and pleased to see her. When she confided in her mother that she had a white boyfriend, she did not like it at all, saying that to her that amounted to prostitution. Evbu smiled and soothed her mother, explaining to her why it had been a convenient arrangement.

'Well,' said Evbu's mother, 'your father is watching over us all and, as you were his favourite child, he will guide you specially. I have no fear.'

There were several letters from Jide. He was happy at Ibadan but missed her. He was going to stop work at the end of August and come to Benin and spend a week there. They would both go back to Lagos together. Evbu longed to see him. It was a pity she could not share her experience in London with him, but she knew that he held all expatriates in contempt because of what was happening in South Africa.

As before, Jide stayed with Henry, but was at Evbu's most of the day. There was no need for secrecy this time. Evbu's family liked him, but secretly her mother wished she would not marry him. Jide was too good-looking for his own good, she thought, and that he looked like a womaniser, too.

From all indications he was extremely fond of Evbu, but that did not prevent him from giving Izogie the eye when they were all sitting in the parlour with some visitors some days before. Evbu herself had noticed it and had frowned. Idemudia and Nosawaru had thought it fun watching the little drama.

When they both got back to Lagos, Jide delved straight into his studies and Evbu again began the arduous task of looking for a job. She had thought it would be quite easy, given her qualifications, but it was not like that. Most companies preferred secretaries with at least two years' experience, and already working for a reputable company.

Evbu became weary and confused about the whole thing. Jide was too involved in his studies to offer any useful advice and she was getting tired of showing her certificates and giving her life history to every personnel officer she came across. One morning, while waiting for a bus to go and chase an advert she had seen in the papers the previous day, a white Mercedes car stopped some distance away from her and the driver got out and walked up to her.

'Good morning, madam. My Oga wan speak to you.'

'Who is your Oga?'

'He dey that car over dere. We wan give you lift if you dey go our way.'

'Oho!'

Evbu had been waiting for more than an hour for a bus and she could not afford a taxi. She felt there was nothing to lose by accepting a lift during the day. She could always scream for help if there was foul play. She followed the man to the car.

'Good morning, young lady,' said a short, plump man with a round happy face. He was about fifty and was expensively dressed; his clothing suggested that he was either from eastern or mid-western Nigeria. He had a confident air about him.

Can we give you a lift anywhere? I used to be a boy scout and I make it a point of duty to do one good deed a day,' he said smiling. 'We are going to my office at the Marina. Will it help if we drop you there?'

'Good morning, sir,' said Evbu courteously. 'It would be a great help. Actually, I'm going to the Marina too.

'Good! Get in the back with me then.' Thank you, sir."

I'm Chief Odie, Managing Director of Odie and Sons Limited. We are in the construction business. Here's my card."

I'm pleased to meet you, sir. I'm Evbu Isibor.' Are you new in Lagos? I've never seen you at that bus stop. I am very observant and I know the regulars. I have been plying this route most mornings for the past seven years now. Maybe you've just moved to this area?'

No. I have only just finished from College. I schooled in Yaba."

'Ah. Do you work this way, then?'

'No, as a matter of fact, I'm looking for a job. It's proving difficult.'

Have you not been offered anything at all?'

'I have been, twice, but as a shorthand typist. I want a job as a secretary or junior secretary because I have the requisite qualifications.'

'You speak like my eldest daughter. When she makes up her mind what to have, that's what she must have. What are your speeds?'

'100/50."

"That's not bad at all. I know girls with 80/40 who are secretaries. What would you say if I say I have a job to offer you?'

'Oh, that would be very nice, sir,' said Evbu, smiling shyly. 'I work hard although I have no experience.'

"That's good. You will not even have to work hard.'

'But you don't know anything about me, sir. I mean I er, er, have no references or anything.

'Don't worry, Evbu. You look like a well-bred girl and I can always fire you if I am not satisfied with your work and behaviour.'

Evbu was a bit frightened. The man looked soft but sounded tough.

'How old are you?" "Twenty-three, sir.'

'Are your parents here?'

'No, I live with my sister and her husband. Evbu did not want him to think she was a 'loose girl' living alone.

'Fine! Here we are! Come along to my office and meet my other two secretaries. You will replace one who has just left to get married. Driver, take the car to the car park and at eleven go back to the house. I think madam wants to use the car for shopping.'

'Yes, sir.' 'Come along, my dear."

They entered a building and took the lift to the eighth floor. It was a modern air-conditioned building. The Chief's offices were modernly furnished too. There was a large panelled office for the Managing Director, a smaller one shared by the three secretaries, a large one used as general office where there were clerks, typists etc..., then there was a small room where the Chief had his lunch when he was very busy and did not want to go out, and which would be used by his son when he joined his father's business.

Chief Odie or the 'Chief' as he was popularly refer- red to by his workers, introduced Evbu to his other secretaries, Pat and Kemi. Pat was a tall, not too slim girl like Evbu, but she was light in complexion and had long thick hair. Kemi on the other hand was black, of average height and with a good figure. Both girls were attractive and well-dressed. They received Evbu warmly. It was to Kemi that Evbu was easily drawn. She could see that Kemi was friendly by nature and did not seem to think that Evbu was a threat. Pat was friendly enough, but Evbu was sure that she was the jealous type by the way she took in her dress, shoes, make-up and hair as soon as she entered the room. The Chief told Pat to take her to the general office and introduce her to the rest of the staff. After this, Evbu went back to the Chief's office to discuss the salary and her duties.

After a week at the job, Evbu had still not put many of her skills into practice but she saw a lot of the Chief. He did not behave indecently towards her but, each time he had visitors, he would call her into his office on one flimsy excuse or the other. Sometimes he would ask her to join him and his guests for lunch at a nearby restaurant.

At first Evbu thought that this would bring about a certain coolness in her relationship with Pat and Kemi, since girls were usually jealous about such things. But to her surprise, nothing like that happened. They seemed quite satisfied and happy. They did not lack admirers as most of the Chief's guests called at the secretaries' office to say 'hello'. Pat and Kemi always greeted these men familiarly and sometimes they even used their first names.

One day, as they were waiting for the bus after work, Kemi asked her how she liked the job.

'Oh, not bad, but it is terribly boring to sit at the typewriter all day with nothing to do. At this rate I shall forget all I learnt at school."

'You've just left school, then?'

'Yes.'

"That's a pity. You might lose your speed.' "That's what I'm afraid of."

'Why don't you enroll at one of these evening schools for advanced students? It does not cost much, and you might even improve. After spending some time with us here, you can leave for a better job claiming that you have "experience"."

'You seem to understand what my problem is, Kemi. Thanks for the advice. For how long have you and Pat been working for the Chief?'

'I have been working here for more than three years now. I think Pat has been here for about five years or more. We share a flat in Yaba. She is, by the way, the Chief's blue-eyed girl. They come from the same place."

'Don't you get bored working here?"

'Oh, no! Pat and I can hardly type although we are referred to as secretaries. Most of the serious work is carried on in the general office by the typists and clerks. I think the secretaries should actually be referred to as "hostesses".'

'Hostesses!'

'Well, that's the way I see it. You see, the Chief is a contractor of all sorts. He supplies local labour for construction companies and, in his own interest, he tries to help these companies get contracts. He also uses his influence on the firms or corporations giving out these contracts to urge the construction company involved to make use of his services. This is where we come in. He gives parties for the important people in these ventures, we act as hostesses, and sort of follow up in our own way to help push the deal through. It's a lot of fun really.'

"The Chief must have a lot of influence."
'Oh, yes, he does."

'Has he ever dated you or Pat? I'm sorry if this is a personal question. You don't need to answer.'

'I don't mind. At the onset he dated me, and I think he still dates Pat once in a while, but he is like a father to us. I doubt if he dates or would like to date secretaries now. He surely did not date Nkechi, the girl you've replaced. Has he tried to date you?' 'No. I've had lunch with him and some of his friends several times but that's all.'

'He was just trying to show you off. He is very nice, you know, quite generous and sympathetic. He pays for our flat, and he has promised us small cars if we continue to work well and if business is good. Mind you goodness only knows when he will ever admit that business is good!"

One day, Evbu had a letter from Pete. In it he said that he had been taken off the African section of his firm and he was being posted back to Australia. He would miss her and Nigeria terribly, and he hoped that one day in the future he would have the opportunity of coming back to Lagos for a visit. He wished her and Jide good luck and hoped, if they did get married, that it would be a success.

He enclosed a cheque for a large sum which he said was his parting gift. Evbu was grateful for the money, but she knew that she would miss Pete with his ready humour and wit. It was as if a chapter of her life had closed.

Six months after she had started working for the Chief, he gave one of his parties. Evbu was very excited. She loved parties but, when she told Jide of the forthcoming party, he was not enthusiastic. In fact he had never liked the idea of her working for the Chief-more especially when she had told him what Kemi had said about the social side of the job. 'I can't see what your problem is. You have good qualifications and yet you are content to work in a place where you cannot practise what you've been taught. Your boss is a dirty old man who wants to corrupt young ladies. You should resign, if for nothing else, for your own self-respect."

'But I just can't walk out of a job when I don't have another one lined up. What shall I do for money? I know that you've qualified now and are earning some money, but can you look after both of us? I need the job, you know.'

'I can pay your rent and give you pocket money until you get a suitable job."

'What guarantee have I that the next job will not be worse than this? I shall be looking for a job, but I don't want to quit this one yet.'

'I take it that you enjoy the duties you perform for the Chief. I can't stand the thought of old men pawing over you. Send in your letter of resignation on Monday, and come straight back home. After all, you did not sign any bond with him.'

'I didn't, but I can't just walk out on the man like that. He gave me a job when I badly needed one. I can't let him down like that. That would be irresponsible.'

'But you've just told me that there is hardly any work for you to do. How can you let him down when you are idle all the time?'

'I don't want to label myself as unreliable and inconsiderate.'

'I think you're sweet on the old man. Admit it. There's more between both of you than you've told me.'

'Jide, how can you be so hurtful? You know I love no one else but

you.'

'Do you? I have been too busy reading all these years to keep an eye on you. You've changed considerably since we first met. How have you come by all those pretty dresses you've been wearing for the past three years if you don't have a sugar daddy? I'm not that stupid, you know. I have no hold on you but I expect you to be honest with me.'

'What about you? Do you think I have heard nothing about you? A former classmate of mine told me she saw you last month at the beach, arm in arm with another girl. You explain that to me.'

'Your friend was just being malicious. I went to the beach with a couple of friends, but there were no girls with us.'

'I don't believe you. Have I not seen you getting girls' addresses at parties when you thought I wasn't looking? What about your campus? Don't you have girlfriends there? I'm not stupid either!'

'Very well, believe what you like and stick to your sugar daddy. Goodbye! I hate stubborn girls!"

'Please yourself."

As soon as Jide left, Evbu broke down and wept. Jide was always so selfish! How could she stay at home without a job, waiting for him to hand down money to her? Such money she was quite sure would be quite small considering how thrifty he was! Apart from that it would be boring staying at home with nothing to do. Jide did not even care whether she lived in a hole or not. He had been given a flat by the hospital he worked for, but he had not suggested she share it with him.

True, her pictures were all over the flat, but he had hinted in a subtle way that she should visit only when he called for her. His excuse was that his parents might call at any time and he did not want to give the impression that a girlfriend had a key to the flat. What had stopped him introducing her to the parents, anyway?

She had guessed that he must be dating other girls and did not want a clash at his flat. She had not accused him about it because she had no proof and she was still dating Pete at the time. All that had stopped now and there was just Jide. But if she had to stay at home and start all over again to look for a job and be told that she had no experience, then... And now, Jide is gone. Perhaps forever. Her heart ached.

But early next morning there was a knock at the door and Jide came bursting in. They rushed into each other's arms.

'Evbu, my love. I'm sorry I behaved like I did last night. I was consumed with jealousy. You may not believe me, but I love you very much. I could not sleep all night. I thought you might not want to speak to me ever again. We've never had such a quarrel before. If you want to go on working for the Chief for the time being, it's alright by me. We shall both start looking for another job for you.

I shall tell friends to help. I agree with you. It would be unethical and impractical to walk out on him just like that. Give me a kiss now. Say you still love me."

'I shall never stop loving you, Jide.' 'Famous words!"

'Well, I mean them.' 'You don't know how happy you've made me, Evbu. It will take a lot to stop me loving you."

After Jide left, Evbu sat in thought. Could he be playing a game with her? There was no doubt they loved each other, but why had he never mentioned marriage? She had half expected him to ask her that morning. It was fishy the way he had kept their relationship from his people. One of these days she would pay him a surprise visit and find out things for herself.

The Chief's party went very much as Evbu had expected. Once she overcame her initial nervousness she discovered that it was really quite pleasant to play the role of a sophisticated hostess, entertaining important people who wanted nothing more than quiet conversation and a steady supply of food and drink. Evbu was exhilarated when she eventually left to join Jide who was waiting to take her home. Jide was in the garden of the hotel. He was sitting alone, staring morosely in front of him. She was surprised to find him thus, for he was gregarious by nature and usually found a friend to keep him company anywhere. She went behind him and nibbled his ear. He jumped up, startled.

'You were a long time coming. Did you enjoy the party?'

'How could I when you weren't there with me?' she teased. 'Besides, my shoes were too tight and so you can imagine what I went through.'

'I got jealous thinking of you at that party without me,' said Jide seriously. 'I resisted the urge to gatecrash.'

'Ha! Ha! You would have been welcomed.'

She then narrated all that went on at the party. 'Darling, can you see now that this confirms all my fears? The man expects you girls to behave like some cheap whores. You should think again of leaving his employment. I hate this type of life for you, my love. What about if one of these men gets interested in you and you fail to respond? He would report you to the Chief and you would be sacked anyway. Which is more honourable? To resign or to be thrown out?'

'Easy Jide, darling. There's no need for another quarrel on this matter. The Chief must have noticed that I am not interested in such things. He has not forced me to date anyone yet."

'He might if it is important to his business.' 'But Jide, if you care so much about me, why don't we get married? I'm not good enough for you, is that it?'

'Evbu. It's just that I have only recently qualified and I cannot afford to get married yet." 'Can't we get engaged? You've not introduced me to any of your relations yet."

'I hate long engagements. Besides, what does an engagement signify anyway! It's just a mere formality. It does not stop us being unfaithful to each other if we want to be. Even marriage cannot stop that. The important thing is what we feel for each other. As for meeting my people, there's plenty of time for that. Introducing you to them means nothing.

You know I love you more than anyone else in the world. You cannot say that you are not aware of that." In the face of such eloquence and reasonable talk, Evbu did not know what to say next. When a man has declared over and over again how much he loves you, it seems silly to keep whining about engagements and introductions to relations. So there the matter rested for the meantime.

Chapter 5

Evbu had been working for the Chief for almost three years when she saw the following advertisement in one of the dailies:

'Experienced Secretary (male or female) to work for the Chairman/Managing Director of a long established clearing and forwarding company. Must have good speeds-120/60 or 100/50, and be ready to work under stress. Should be of a cheerful disposition and be capable of working without supervision.

Age group-25 to 35. Salary-attractive and negotiable according to qualifications and experience.

Fringe benefits-car loan, housing allowance, etc. Send your applications with

Photostat copies. She showed the advert to Jide and they decided that she should apply without delay. Evbu carried the paper with her for about a week before she plucked up the courage to apply. Jide was surprised and asked her why.

'I know I don't stand a chance, because even though my speeds are good, thanks to my evening classes, I really don't have adequate knowledge of office procedure, so how can I become a Managing Director's secretary?"

'You underestimate yourself, darling, and you are a bit too honest to survive. You won't tell them you have no experience if you are invited for an interview. All you say is that you've been working as a secretary for Chief Odie for more than two years and that you wanted a change. The important thing is that you have good and genuine certificates. The job is within your scope. Tell them you are twenty-eight years old, and try to behave in a cool and mature manner.'

'Well, I have not been called for an interview yet, so I need not fret. I'm sure they will not call me.'

'I'll be surprised if they don't,' said Jide. Sure enough, two weeks after she sent in her application Evbu went for an interview.

She dressed simply for the interview with the Managing Director. She wore a brown skirt and a silk short-sleeved shirt in cream. She made her hair carefully, and wore matching shoes and a handbag. She decided not to use any make-up. She did not want to give the man the impression that she was a tart by appearing overdressed and made up. When she looked in the mirror she saw a cool, efficient secretary staring back at her.

'Well, that ought to make a good impression on the blighter, whoever he is.'

The Personnel Officer smiled approvingly when he saw her. 'Right on time. That's good. The MD will be pleased. Let's go. They first went to the MD's Secretary's office where a typist, who was holding the fort, told them that the MD was seeing a visitor off and had said that Mr Afolabi (the Personnel Officer) and the new secretary should wait in the office.

They went in and sat down. It was a big room with lovely office furniture and a thick carpet which matched the comfortable visitors' settees. There was a sweet fragrance in the cool air, and Evbu suspected that the room had just been sprayed with air freshener. Everywhere was clean and the desk was tidy with everything in its place. She could not help wondering how she would cope if given a job considering how meticulous the MD seemed to be. She tried to imagine how he looked-probably short and fat and very neat. The type of boss who would read the notes you have taken in shorthand and would point out wrong outlines! She became very nervous.

Shortly, the other door opened and an attractive and well-dressed lady in her forties walked briskly in and Mr Afolabi stood up.

'Good morning, Mrs Niyi. This is Miss Evbu Isibor, the lady who has come for the post of your secretary.'

'Oh, yes,' said the lady. 'Please sit down."

Evbu stood for some seconds longer as if in a daze. She never expected that the Managing Director of such an important company would be a lady.

'Please sit down, Miss Isibor. I guess you are surprised to know that a woman is the

Managing Director. People always are the first time they come into my office.'

'I'm sorry, Madam. I didn't mean to stare, it's just that it came as a surprise.'

'Yes, I know. It's time we women showed the men that we are just as good as they are in business, if not better, isn't it Mr Afolabi?'

'Quite true, Mrs Niyi. "What a man can do a woman can do even better" used to be a popular debate topic during my Secondary School days."

'During mine, too. We used to have a great time in our school discussing ways in which women did better than men in all aspects of life. Well, now to business. Miss Isibor, from your documents here, I see that you have had two years' experience working as a secretary for the same person."

'Yes, I have been working for Chief Odie since I left school.'

'Could you tell me a bit about your duties in the office?'

'Well, there are the usual secretarial duties-taking notes, typing, filing, answering and making telephone calls and generally looking after the boss's affairs in the office. There are outside engagements as well, like going after the suppliers and seeing that deliveries are made on time, etc. Even when my boss goes on tour, there is still a lot of work for me to do.'

'Hmm! I see. So, you are used to working on your own when your boss is away?'.
'Yes. I don't need any supervisor once I get the hang of the job."

'You sound confident. I have met Chief Odie briefly several times. He belongs to the same club as my husband. From what I've heard, he is quite a strict man. So, if you've been in his employment and worked closely with him for two years, then you must have something to offer. Ah, here is the Chief's letter of recommendation. Hm, that's good. When can you start here?'

'Within two weeks, Madam, if that's alright with you and if we agree on the fringe benefits and conditions of service.'

'Fair enough! You deal with Mr Afolabi about that. By the way, Mr Afolabi, are there any more candidates I have to see?'

'Yes. Two more this afternoon.'

'Well, you deal with them. I'm satisfied with Miss Isibor's performance at the interview and I'm willing to have her as my secretary. If she refuses our offer, then I suppose I'll have to see the others even though I have a tight schedule today. Miss Isibor, good day.'

'Good day, Madam,' said Evbu standing up. "Thank you.'

After having a detailed talk with the Personnel Officer, Evbu accepted the job and was told to come and start the following week. She was jubilant. She left the office and took a taxi to the Teaching Hospital where she left a note with the receptionist for Jide, telling him of the good news. She felt she could not wait until he called in the evening.

She then went down into a Post Office and wrote a hurried note to her mother informing her of her change of job and giving the address of her new place of work. They always shared good news in the family. She knew that her mother, brothers and sisters would rejoice with her for landing a good job.

When Jide did not call that evening as he had promised, Evbu was worried. He usually kept his promises. He was just as anxious as she was to know the outcome of the interview. She could not imagine what could have kept him- perhaps an emergency. A doctor has to be prepared for that.

Next day, whan Pat and Kemi were out for lunch, Evbu decided to ring Jide up at his flat to find out if he was alright. She reasoned that if he had worked throughout the previous night, he would be 'off' the next day. She was surprised when a lady answered at the other end, and she could not help asking, 'Who's that?'

'What do you mean, who's that?' answered the voice. 'Do you ring up people to ask who they are?'

'Oh, I'm sorry! I guess I must have dialled the wrong number."

"This is extension 050-Teaching Hospital.'

"That was the extension I wanted. Can I speak to Jide, please? Is he in?'

'Who are you?'

'I beg your pardon! Isn't that Jide Jones' flat? I should ask you who you are, madam.'

'Why? Anyway, I'm Dr Shade Bayo, Jide's fiancée. Now, who are you?'

'You are Jide's what?' gulped Evbu, and the phone dropped from her hand. When she replaced it Shade had already dropped hers. Who could the girl be? Wondered Evbu wildly. It was one thing to hear rumours, but it was another thing to be confronted by the real thing. She had never had such a challenge in all the years of her relationship with Jide. Dr Shade Bayo. She just did not know what to think or feel. If only she could get in touch with Jide right then!

She knew it was useless going to the Teaching Hospital to check. Could it have been a joke? Could Jide have been there by the girl? Perhaps he would ring later to say it was a joke. Not that he indulged in such things, knowing how painful it would be to her. Perhaps it was his sister or something. She decided to confide in Kemi.

Kemi used to have a doctor boyfriend at the Teaching Hospital and knew everyone. She might have heard of Dr Shade Bayo. Shade on the other hand guessed it was Evbu who had telephoned. She had no doubt about that. No other girl would dare ask who was at the other end of the telephone. Certainly not the student nurses that Jide fooled around with. If any of them heard her voice on the line, they would feverishly drop the telephone.

Jide had told her about Evbu, and she had been clever enough to know that it was wiser to try and win her way into his heart by not setting up herself outright as Evbu's rival. She had no doubt at all that Jide would abandon Evbu sooner or later, for he was one of those men who cared about connections with wealthy and popular families, like hers. She knew that he would rather have a doctor for a wife than a nondescript secretary. She had tolerated Evbu's photographs for some time around the flat and then, after creating the right mood, she gently told Jide that the photographs were better put in the album where they would not be so conspicuous.

She said that when her friends came with her to Jide's flat, they usually asked if that was his wife. It embarrassed her sometimes. He agreed, and the photographs were put in an album, where Shade promptly destroyed them without telling him. That afternoon, when Pat went out for an outside assignment, Evbu confided in Kemi. She knew that she was a gossip, but all the same, she needed to tell someone.

'Kemi,' said Evbu later that afternoon, 'I need your advice. I have been terribly upset since I got some news this afternoon.' 'Poor you!' sympathised with Kemi. 'Good news yesterday, bad news today. Never mind! That's the way of the world. What do you want my advice about?'

Evbu burst into tears and narrated what had taken place earlier. 'Goodness, Evbu! You mean you don't know about Shade Bayo and Jide? Pat and I have run into them at parties several times during the past year. I thought you knew and did not mind. They are not officially engaged, but Shade spends most of her time with Jide, or at least in his flat. Have you never met her in his flat?'

'No, I hardly ever go there. We usually meet in my house. He does take me to his flat sometimes, but I don't go there on my own.'

'Why not?'

'Jide doesn't seem to like it. He has never actually said so but, from his reaction when I once went there on my own without informing him, I guessed he did not like it. I hate not being welcomed.'

'I understand. That's pride. You don't want to be shunned or to catch him red-handed with other girls, or did you not know that he is a terrible flirt?'

'I know that he flirts like other single young men, but there has never been any particular girl he was attached to except me. I thought he was sowing his wild oats.'

'Yet he has a key to your room and can visit you without notice. Shade obviously has a key to his flat. You, who have been his girlfriend for some six years or more, do not have a key to his flat and cannot visit him whenever you wish. Now, you tell me. Why bother about him? He is not the dishiest guy around. He is quite nice and popular and handsome, but if after all these years you cannot visit him freely then what are you wasting your time with him for?'

'Kemi, you don't understand. I really love him, you know! It was because of him that I came to Lagos in the first place.'

'Has he ever introduced you to his family? Abeokuta is not all that far from Lagos. Has he taken you there for a weekend, or introduced you to the people who matter to him?'

'No.'

'Well, I can assure you that he has taken Shade. I understand that she even sends presents to his mother and sisters. When the sisters came to Lagos during the last holiday, they went shopping with Shade.'

'How did you know all this?'

'I came from Abeokuta too-Shade's family is well-known there. She comes from a big family full of lawyers, doctors, engineers, the lot. Although we are not acquaintances, we say "hello" to each other at parties. She is not aware that you are my col- league and friend. She knows about you, of course."

'Why didn't you or Pat warn me about Jide and Shade right from the onset? That was disloyal of you both. I would not treat you like that. You know how I feel about Jide.'

'Yes, we know, darling. We are sorry, but you see, we debated for several days whether to tell you or not, but decided against telling you in the end. We thought that you probably have someone back home in Benin City that you want to marry, and are probably playing around with Jide just like he is doing with you, although we are quite aware that you are both terribly fond of each other. You know how it happens sometimes-you carry on a passionate relationship with someone, but when you want to settle down for marriage you do so with someone else.

Moreover, we had seen you twice at the "Crab" with another man."

Evbu was dumbfounded! 'You never mentioned it to me,' she said weakly.

"There was no point. Pat and I were there with some foreign boyfriends and we were not anxious that you should see us.'

'Well,' laughed Evbu, 'it takes a thief to catch a thief!'

'Oh, well, such is life."

'What should I do about Jide? I'm angry and disappointed. I have a good mind to go straight to the Hospital after work and force him and Shade to a showdown.'

'What will you gain from that? He may love you but can you predict what his reaction will be if faced with such a scene? Never force a showdown with a boyfriend or husband in the presence of a rival. If the rival is sensible, she will keep quiet and act the hurt and innocent party. That will swing the man's sympathy to her side. He might even take sides with her and tell you off. The best thing is to wait until he calls at your place, then you can have a jolly good scream at him. Take advice from an experienced girl.'

'Experienced girl, indeed! You are not much older than I am. In fact, sometimes, I even believe that I'm older than you are."

'Oh no, you're not,' laughed Kemi. 'I was thirty earlier this year. I have been married twice, and I have three kids who live with my mother in Abeokuta.'

'Really?' gasped Evbu. 'You don't look it.'

'Well, I sincerely hope not, otherwise I would begin to think that all the beauty treatments I have been having from salons have been in vain. I have seen something of life. I advise you to ask Jide calmly when next you see him. Don't fly into a rage or weep. Just make him tell you everything. From what he says, you will be able to deduce whether you have a future with him or not.'

"Thank you, Kemi. What you've just said makes sense. It won't be easy, but I'll try to be calm.'

After work that day Evbu took a taxi home, not minding the cost. She felt she was in no mood to queue for a bus. Her heart ached whenever she thought of the fact that Jide might actually want to marry another girl. After all these years! She felt as if her world was about to collapse. She was almost tempted not to ask him about Shade, but rather to continue to believe that she was the only girl who mattered to him. That would probably be the best thing to do! How could Jide possibly want someone else for a wife? In her heart of hearts, though, she knew nothing was impossible when it came to the question of love.

On getting home, she collected herself and set about preparing Jide's favourite meal of rice and fish stew. All the while she kept thinking of what her opening line should be. She would have preferred to take hold of his shirt or tie as soon as he set foot in the room, demanding to know what the game was. That way, she would be able to show all her pent up feelings. But Kemi had said that that was not the best approach.

Well, one thing she was sure of was that she would show Jide that she was more attractive than Shade-whatever she looked like. She would show Jide what he would miss if he left her. She decided that she would have a nice bath and then dress the way he liked her to.

When she got back from the bathroom, she found Jide waiting for her. As soon as he saw her, he jumped up and gathered her in his arms.

'Hmmmmmm . . . darling, you smell nice and fresh,' he said, kissing her. As usual when he kissed her, Evbu melted and returned his kiss. She found it difficult to think that this was the man who was contemplating marriage with some other girl.

'How did the interview go?"

'Wait, let me get dressed, and I will tell you about it.'

'Not on your life! You're okay the way you are, and I'm anxious to hear everything. Sit on my lap and shoot.' Evbu laughed nervously and sat on his lap. Then she told him about the interview.

'Well,' he said when she had finished, 'this calls for lots of kisses and a celebration. We shall go out right away.'

'Why did you not come yesterday as you had promised?'

'Darling, I was coming to that. I had to stand in for another doctor who was sick, and I was told at the last minute. Was I furious! I was kept busy all through the night and there was no way I could reach you. I thought you would ring me up today to ask what had happened. I was pretty disappointed when you did not. I asked the receptionist if I had any message and she said that I had none.'

'But I left a note with the receptionist for you yesterday. I wanted you to be the first to hear the news, so I went all the way from Lagos to Idi-Araba just to tell you.'

'I was not given the note. It probably got lost, or it might be in my pigeon hole. I have not checked my letters for days now.'

'Check tomorrow. I will throw some clothes on and we will have dinner before going out."

'Did you prepare dinner? I thought we could go out tonight for a meal. All the same I would hate to waste what you've specially prepared for me. What is it?'

'Your favourite.'

'Good girl.'

They ate and Evbu went to dress for the evening out. She took her time about it and emerged looking very gorgeous in a long and clinging mauve dress. Jide whistled when he saw her.

'Sweetheart, you look fabulous and I'm madly in love with you,' he said tenderly and seriously as he took her in his arms. 'Don't ever think of leaving me for some other man. That would mess up my whole life. Sometimes, I wonder how I can bear to leave you here and live elsewhere.'

'If you feel like that, then who is the girl girl.... began Evbu and then checked herself.

'What girl? Look, darling, there's no other girl I love but you, no matter what other people say. I have fun, as you are well aware, but I'm no different from other boys. As I told you when we first got acquainted, all these girls mean nothing to me. Let's not spoil the evening, my love. This is your big night. Just command and your wish will be done. Shall we go to the pictures first and then see what else we want to do? I don't have to go on duty until tomorrow evening, so it does not matter if I go to bed at six in the morning.'

'Fine, but I have to be at the office at eight." 'Oh, that office! Never mind, you'll soon work in a proper office.'

'You and your prejudice,' laughed Evbu.

They went to the pictures but hardly glanced at the screen. In between kissing and cuddling, they kept up a steady flow of conversation in low voices, to the annoyance of other spectators who wanted to concentrate on the film. Evbu wondered how she was going to steer the conversation to the more serious topic of Jide's relationship with Shade when they were in such a loving mood. She really felt a lot of love in her heart for him, and she could tell too that he felt the same. They were not just acting. When they left the cinema house, Jide drove around for some time while they decided where to go.

In the end he stopped abruptly outside 'The Crab'. The moment the bouncer at the club winked at her as they entered, Evbu knew that it was a mistake to have allowed Jide to bring her there. Not that she could have helped it since they did not discuss it beforehand. He had actually parked the car before she realised where they really were, and it would have been suspicious to have made such a fuss about not wanting to go in.

Two years before, she and Pete had been pretty frequently there whenever he was in town. He had liked "The Crab' best of all the night clubs in Lagos because he said the atmosphere and music reminded him of the Caribbean countries which he loved very much.

The Lebanese manager, Richy, who ran the club, was his personal friend. Evbu had not been to the club since Pete stopped coming to Nigeria. Now, she felt like running out of it. She just prayed silently that she would not be recognised by Richy or the waiters in the dim light. She and Jide sat at an empty table and ordered drinks. She looked round furtively and could not see Richy anywhere. Thank goodness for that! Perhaps he had left the country and the club was now in the hands of someone else.

There were still a few of the old waiters left, but she refused to meet their eyes as they took the orders and brought them their drinks, and after some time she began to relax. She and Jide chatted and danced. It was all so romantic and tender although she could not get Shade out of her mind.

Later, as she and Jide were talking tête-à-tête someone came and clasped him on the shoulders.

'JJ, old boy,' he said. 'Oh, hello, Evbu, you are looking cool as usual. Lucky guy, Jide.'

Evbu looked up and recognised Akpan, one of Jide's schoolmates at King's College.

'Hello, Akpan,' greeted Jide and Evbu.

'What are you doing here?' asked Jide. 'I thought your eyes shut at 9.30 pm prompt every day, after the news on the telly. Don't tell me you've changed since I last saw you.'

'Well, I have found the love of a great woman and...

'What! Another one! You were enjoying the love of a great one only three months ago.'

'Oh, that! You must be referring to Sandra, or was it Tinu or Pat? Anyway, that's history. This is the real thing, man. Her name is Marianne. Come and meet her. She's cool, man.'

'Hm! You watch it or she will really succeed in dragging you to the altar and the bachelor circle will suffer the loss of the decade.'

'No fear, sir. I shall be willing this time. Come along! I don't like to leave her for too long. Other men might get ideas. Evbu, please excuse us.' "That's alright, Akpan,' said Evbu, smiling. 'I'll be right back, darling,' called Jide.

Evbu ordered another drink and began to take in the scene. Most of the girls there were strangers to her, and they looked quite young and sophisticated. She wondered where the old regulars were. Probably at some other joint or possibly they had given up the trade. She felt an inward glow of satisfaction that she didn't need to go round night clubs anymore.

Just then, Richy walked into the club, looked round, saw Evbu and made straight for her table.

'Hello E, darling,' he said, kissing her fondly on the cheek. You look grand. Long time no see! I thought that the Club had lost one of its favourite couples! Is Pete here with you? I haven't seen him for a long time now,' he concluded, placing an arm on Evbu's shoulders.

Evbu gasped and looked ill. Right behind Richy stood Jide, watching with a puzzled expression on his face. All sorts of wild thoughts came into Evbu's mind. She felt as if the floor should open up and swallow her up. Things were happening too fast for her. Richy on the other hand was amazed at Evbu's confusion. He knew that she was not one to rush into your arms and kiss you affectionately, but she usually returned his greetings warmly whenever she and Pete called at the club.

'E, what's the matter?' he asked. He had never succeeded in pronouncing her name properly, so he had settled for the first letter. 'Are you sick?' He persisted when Evbu remained silent. Jide then stepped forward.

'Can I help you, sir?' he asked Richy. 'Evbu is with me.'

'Oh!' said Richy as realisation hit him. It was silly of him to assume that Evbu would call at the club only with Pete. 'No, no, I made a mistake. Look, can I buy you both a drink? I'm Richy, I run this club.' 'No, thank you,' Jide said coldly. He hated all these foreign nightclub owners who were only in the country to fill their pockets. 'Please leave us. Evbu, drink up and let's go. Let's go and sit in the garden for a while.'

They pushed their way out into the garden. It was almost deserted. Later, it would be full when people would be trying to make arrangements for the night. Jide led Evbu to a stone table and they both sat down. 'Would you like a drink?' he asked. 'No,' answered Evbu in a small voice.

'Alright, please tell me what a Lebanese was doing kissing you fondly and calling you "darling". Who was his friend Pete that he referred to?'

Jide did not believe in beating about the bush. Before Evbu could say anything, he continued, 'I would appreciate it very much if you told me the truth, Evbu. I don't want to be forced to go and make my own investigations. Tell me the truth and I will accept it no matter how bitter. I love you and that's all that matters for now. Don't let a lie destroy what we feel for each other.'

Encouraged by the tenderness in his voice, Evbu told him about how she was hard up for money and had dated Pete. Jide allowed her to finish and then he slapped her hard twice. This attracted the attention of the couple who were on the other side of the garden.

'You cheap filthy whore,' he exploded. 'Fancy you going with non-blacks of all people.

You know full well what I think of them and how I loathe and despise them for what they are doing to our race all over the world. I would not have minded much if you had a sugar daddy or something, but them! Goodness, I must be going crazy. To think that I have wasted years loving you, thinking that one day we would get married and ...

That did it! Evbu came out of her stupor. 'Marry!' she hissed at him. 'You never intended to marry me in your life, you selfish flirt! What about Shade Bayo? She lives in your flat doesn't she? You think that I don't know about her? You're scheming son-of-a-bitch! What do you know about life? I did what I did because I came from a poor family and wanted to get educated.

You have no excuse for luring me from Benin City and then ditching me to go and get engaged to another girl just because she is a doctor and comes from the same village as you. You've cheated on me with other girls too, but I didn't mind because I thought you were sowing your wild oats.

If you actually cared about me, you would have helped me with my school fees. You talk about Pete. He was kind and sympathetic to me and did not despise me. You are nothing but a hypocrite, Jide Jones. What have I done that is so strange that it has been unheard of?'

'Anyway, just get out of my life,' said Jide, recovering fast from his surprise that his relationship with Shade was no longer a secret to Evbu. 'If you want to know,' he said, wanting to hurt Evbu even further, 'Shade is worth a thousand of you, and I shall marry her as soon as possible.'

'Good luck to both of you,' screamed
Evbu, past caring now about the onlookers who
craved to hear every word. 'I hope you will ask
all your other girlfriends to be bridesmaids and
hostesses. It is only fair that the church or
reception hall should be filled with your lovers.'
This drew sniggers from the watchers.

'I jolly well shall,' he retorted as he stood
up. 'Goodbye and goodnight!'

'Aren't you taking me back home?'

'You're joking!' he laughed bitterly.
"Take you back home indeed! Do you imagine
that I would soil my car and myself with you
again? Stick around and pick another Pete. My
God, what an escape!' And with that he strode
off.

Evbu was dumbfounded. She had come
out without any money and there she was
stranded! She ignored the men who were trying

to sidle up to her. She could take a taxi home and pay when she got there, but she did not like the idea of going home alone at that hour. It was rather risky. There was only one thing she could do and that was to go and ask Richy for help.

When Richy saw her come back alone into the club looking dejected he hurried over to her, and began to apologise for the gaff he had committed.

'Don't worry, Richy, you couldn't have known. Let's forget about the whole incident. Could you lend me some money to take a taxi home and also ask one of your boys to accompany me? I shall send the money back through him.'

'Oh, no! The least I can do to make amends is to ask my driver to take you home. Just wait outside. Rashidi, my driver, you remember him, will bring the car round. I'm terribly sorry that I have ruined your evening.'

'You didn't, Richy. What took place was bound to happen sooner or later. Most of it was my fault. Well, thanks for the use of your car. Goodnight.'

'Goodbye.'

When she got home she fell on her bed without bothering to undress. She wept for some time but fell asleep at last.

When Jide left the 'Crab' that night he drove straight to the beach. He needed to clear his head and think. The beach was deserted, but he could hear the waves and the singing of members of the Cherubim and Seraphim sects who were worship- ping in the distance.

Apart from the croaking of frogs in a nearby pond, the splashing of the waves on the shore, and the occasional car, everywhere was still. He felt as if he was in a dream. His darling Evbu! How could she have brought herself so low? Black sugar daddies he could understand and perhaps swallow. It was the fashion these days-even Shade had had some. But foreigners! He had loved her passionately and she had let him down. Her excuse was that she had wanted to get more education. Just that!

He became more and more confused. Perhaps he had been wrong to ditch her at the club. That was ungentlemanly. After all, he had taken her there. He had better go back for her. When he got back to the club, the gateman said on inquiry that she had left. He drove to her house and saw the lights in her room.

'At least she got home safely,' he said to himself. He thought of breaking down the door and giving Evbu a sound beating to relieve himself of his anger, but decided against it. He might end up in jail.

When he got back home, he parked the car but did not go to his flat. He knew that Shade would be there. She was on 'call' that night and she had a key to the flat. He was in no mood to see her. So, instead of going in, he went to the flat above his where Musa, his close friend, lived.

Musa was surprised to find Jide on his doorstep at five in the morning.

'Goodness man, what's the matter? Did Shade push you out of your own flat? Come in and put up your feet. Now, tell "Uncle Musa" everything."

"This is not the time to joke, Musa. My life is in a crisis!'

'Holy Prophet!' cried Musa, impressed. 'What happened?'

'It's Evbu!'

'Now, what have you been doing to the poor girl?" Musa rather liked her. 'Has she found out about Shade? I told you she was bound to, sooner or later. I don't know why you hesitate between the two. It is obvious to everyone where your heart is.' 'Be quiet Musa, and listen to this."

He then narrated what had taken place that evening. When he had finished they both sat there thinking. Then Musa said,

'Where exactly lies your disappointment and anger, Jide? Is it because she dated other men or because these men were expatriates?'

'In both!'

'Fair enough. Now let's analyse this step by step. Why should she not date other people? She was single and was not engaged to you. You had lots of girlfriends. What preferential treatment did you give her? Did you take her to your parents? Did you promise to marry her? Apart from all this, since you know her background very well, why didn't you insist on knowing the source from which she financed her studies? According to what you've just told me,. she said that her reason for picking up men at night- clubs for that brief period was to earn money to see her studies through. For that, I admire her courage and determination. She stopped when she had enough money for her needs.

All this happened a long time ago, and the fact that neither you nor any of your friends came across her in this role shows just how very discreet she was. Poor girl! She must have been through a lot to conceal it.

Frankly, I think she is a nice and respectable girl. I'm not in support of prostitution, but it is something that exists. If this Pete dated her steadily for a year, then it means that he did not consider her a prostitute, but someone who needed help. I don't regard Evbu as a whore. You know very well that some of these girls we admire and date are worse than some of those who frequent clubs.

Remember our third year at the Medical School when that smashing girl in our class made several boys in one of the halls contract venereal disease? We all felt sorry for her then. As for the colour of the men Evbu went with, that's neither here nor there. We all have our prejudices whether tribal, or racial, or otherwise. I abhor apartheid, and I won't look down on a person just because of his colour. Come on man, some of our lecturers were married to expatriates-that did not stop you from going for lectures. I clearly remember you making eyes at the wife of one of them.'

'I know, but if you suddenly discovered that Binta had behaved like Evbu did in the past what would your reaction be?'

'I would be a bit taken aback, but I would go ahead and marry her as we had planned. I would try and understand why she did such a thing. Anyway, I would have been so involved in whatever she was doing that she would not be driven to take such a drastic step. You rather left her to paddle her own canoe and solve her own problems while your nose was in your books.'

'How could I have helped her? I didn't have much money.'

"That's true, but you could have put more effort into helping her get a job. Your uncle and his wife would have helped."

"True. I did not think of that.'

'Anyway, Jide, I think you made a mountain out of a molehill. You are normally a sensible man and, if you think deeply, you will agree with me that you have wronged Evbu. You shouldn't blame her for what she did ages ago. Rather, blame the society which cannot provide education free at all levels.'

'Put like that, I see that I lost control of myself. I ought to apologise to her and beg for forgiveness. I really love that girl, you know. I will buy her favourite perfume and go and make amends this evening. Do you think you can speak to her too, Musa? She likes you a lot and will listen to you. I'm almost afraid to approach her.'

'Wait a minute, Jide. Aren't you rushing things? What plans do you have for Evbu? Are you going to defy your parents and marry a non-Egba girl? What about Shade?'

Jide thought for a while and said slowly, 'No, I don't think I would like to defy my parents and marry against their wishes. I can do what I like and damn the consequences, but it would break their old hearts, and my father would disinherit me. He's done a lot for me-financing my studies, seeing that I had most of the things I wanted, and so on. Shade is the only Egba girl I have shown any interest in so far, so my parents are encouraging the match.'

'Well, there you are! Why make up with Evbu only to break her heart sooner or later? My advice to you is to let the relationship die out now. It would be less painful on both sides in the long run. However, that does not stop you apologising for the way you treated her.'

'I can never get her out of my mind.'

'Don't even try. If you apologise now, then there will be less embarrassment when you meet somewhere someday.'

'I guess you're right. She is so sensitive.' 'Are you going to marry Shade?'

'I guess so.'

'Well, good luck, old boy. She is not bad at all, but remember that we all knew when she was the girl- friend of one of the professors. I don't mean any offence, I just want to remind you so that in future, I will not hold it against her and make her life a misery. It's a pity you cannot marry the girl you really love, but that happens all the time, and you may learn to love Shade as time goes on. Evbu will get a worthy man to marry her. She's a sweet girl. Let's give her some days to cool down, then we shall call on her.'

When Evbu got back to Lagos after a few days holiday in Benin, she was given a lovely send-off party by the Chief and other members of staff. She was touched by the gesture and was surprised that she seemed to be so well-liked by them.

That night she sat alone in her room opening the presents and reading the attached cards. Over the weeks, she got used to being on her own in the evenings. When she got back from Benin, she had seen Jide's note saying that he and Musa had called to apologise for his behaviour. Neighbours had told them that she had travelled out of Lagos.

She decided not to write to Jide, instead she wrote to Musa saying that there was nothing to forgive, and that she wished Jide 'good luck' in all his endeavours, but that she would really be grateful if she were left in peace to pursue her life as she liked. After that, there had been no further communication on either side.

Chapter 6

During the next few weeks Evbu threw herself into her work and had no social life at all for a while. She would stay on after office hours sometimes to do extra work. It was easy for her to work hard because Mrs Niyi herself was a very hard-working lady.

She was overjoyed when she got a letter con- firming her appointment, and giving her a raise.

'Now, I can start looking for a decent place to live in,' she told her friends.

Four months later she finally got a suitable two-bedroom flat with its own kitchen and bathroom. Evbu was very pleased with it. What she liked most was having a bathroom to herself where she could take her bath at leisure without neighbours banging on the door telling her to hurry up.

She was forever cleaning up the place and adding new pieces of furniture to brighten it up. She applied for a car loan and then began to take driving lessons. For the first four months after getting her car she used a driver, until she got her driving licence and was quite confident behind the wheel.

By this time Evbu had developed a very good working relationship with Mrs Niyi. She kept her private life separate from her work. You seldom found her making a personal call, and men never called to see her at work. Yet Mrs Niyi knew that she had boyfriends and that one of them had taken her away for a holiday over the Christmas period. She had seen them together at the movies, but had kept a discreet distance from them. She had never asked her about it, although the women had, in a way, become friends.

Mrs Niyi at home was quite different from the boss in the office. She looked lovelier and more feminine. It was easy to see that Mr Niyi worshipped his family, especially his wife. 'Could he be acting?' thought Evbu. She knew from experience that some men could love their wives and children all their lives and still have affairs on the side. One of her casual boyfriends never stopped talking about his wife and children-how hardworking the wife was and how clever the children were.

Whenever he bought anything for Evbu he always bought things for his family, and sometimes enlisted her help in choosing. It used to amuse her a lot, although she found it all boring after a while. She was not in love with him so jealousy was out of the question. After Jide, she had made up her mind not to get serious with any man, but rather to play the field until she met someone special. She enjoyed every one of these relationships but she made sure that none lasted more than a few months. Some of the married men she dated wanted her to be a second or third wife. They promised her everything-a nice rented flat with servants, a flashy car, a large allowance. She refused.

But the news came that Jide had married Shade, and for a while all the careful control that Evbu had built up around her emotions disintegrated. Once again she felt all the loneliness that had beset her when first Jide had left her, and which none of her casual relationships and friendships, no matter how enjoyable, could prevent her from feeling.

Although outwardly calm and cheerful, Evbu sometimes thought of Jide with a dull ache in her heart. She had not set eyes on him since the day they quarrelled, but Kemi regularly brought her news of him and his family. However, whenever she thought over the last ten years of her life, and took stock of what had taken place, she decided that she had a lot to be thankful for. True that she had lost Jide, but she had achieved part of what she had set out to achieve all those years ago when she had run away on the eve of her wedding to Osaretin. She could lead now the life that she had thought would always be beyond her.

She had a nice job, a car, and she could count several important people among her friends. If she needed a change of job, it would be no problem at all. She had already been offered secretarial positions in other firms, but she enjoyed working for Mrs Niyi, although she knew that she could earn more money elsewhere.

One Saturday afternoon she was having a drink with Kate, an ex-schoolmate of hers, in the gardens of the Harbour Hotel when a familiar voice said, 'Good afternoon, ladies. May I join you?'

Evbu's heart missed a beat when she turned round and saw Jide. He had not changed much at thirty. He looked more mature of course, but he still had the same charming smile and was elegantly dressed. He had kept his figure well too. But Evbu could immediately discern from his eyes that he was not happy. Perhaps he was overworked. She had heard that he was a dedicated doctor.

Kate, on seeing the handsome stranger, quickly said, 'Please join us if you like,' with a winning smile. Evbu, after her initial surprise she kept her eyes averted and said nothing.

Jide ran his eyes over her hungrily. 'Yes,' he said to himself, 'she has not changed one bit. She's just as I imagined she would be. She looks even more at- tractive now she's older.'

He kept staring at her but she refused to meet his eyes. Kate looked from one to the other and decided that something odd was going on that did not involve her.

'Evbu,' she said, 'I promised to meet someone at the swimming pool at five. I will see you later.'

'I'll come with you,' said Evbu, getting up too. 'I think I need a swim.'

'Evbu,' said Jide urgently, 'please stay for a few minutes. I have something to say to you.'

She kept silent.

'Please, Evbu,' insisted Jide. She looked at him briefly.

'Alright,' she said at last. 'Wait for me please, Kate.'

'I'm afraid I can't. It's already ten minutes past five. I hate being late. I'll see you later, darling,' she said and gave Evbu a peck on the cheek, nodded at Jide and left. Evbu and Jide then sat down.

'Evbu, won't you even look at me?' he said, as soon as they were alone.

'Is it important that I should?' "To me, yes."

'What is it you want to say to me?'

"That, that, I'm... er... sorry that we parted." 'Well, that's alright. You said that in our letter over two years ago."

'I know, but I have always wanted to say it in per- son.'

'And now you have. Goodbye."

'Wait Evbu, I have something else to say to you.' 'Now what? I should imagine that a popular doc- tor like you would not want to be seen with an ex- whore like me.'

'Please, Evbu, that's all in the past. I behaved abominably and I hope that, in time, you will learn to forgive me.'

"There's nothing to forgive. You don't owe me anything. You married the girl of your own choice, you now have a daughter and are quite happy, so why bother about whether I forgive you or not?'

'It's because I regret parting from you. I have not found happiness with Shade. Even my parents agree that we are not right for each other.'

"That's a pity, and I'm sorry to hear it, Jide, but why pick me for a confidant? You wanted to marry a girl from your place who was a doctor and you did. Why come and cry on my shoulder? For the sake of the love we once shared, I will always be sorry to know that you're unhappy, but I'm afraid that's all I can do. It's up to you to make your marriage work.'

Jide inwardly doubted the possibility of that. Quarrels over the constant untidiness of the house, irregular meals, and the string of boyfriends Shade had were all he now expected from his marriage. He had not been entirely blameless himself. He had had girlfriends and had been too short-tempered with Shade. He had expected her to be a loving and gentle wife, the type you are glad to come back to at the end of a hard day.

True, she had her job, but it was in order to have a home life of some sort that it was agreed that she should join one of the clinics of a private hospital group, where the hours were less demanding. She worked well and was well-paid. Actually, Jide had been very proud of her until things went sour. He began to notice that, although she left the clinic earlier than some working wives, she was hardly ever at home when he got back, and when he was on night duty, she went off to parties. Bola, their only child, was left to the nanny most of the time.

The trouble with Jide was that he was used to being the main attraction wherever he was-at home with his parents, at the hospital with nurses and patients, at parties with girls-so his ego was somewhat deflated when Shade ceased to worship him at home. Since she had fought tooth and nail to get him to marry her, he had thought she would continue to be humble and clinging, and would accept any treatment meted out to her. On the contrary, she had reared up and demonstrated her intention to share the limelight herself.

At first Jide had been amused, but later on he had resented taking second position in the house, and that was when the quarrels really started. They were awful ones-getting more and more bitter with each saying things that really hurt. They usually made up afterwards but they found themselves drifting apart and seeking solace with others. The arrival of the baby had brought them temporarily together, but very shortly they drifted apart again. Jide might have been more tolerant if he had been in love with Shade, but he was not and the least thing she did angered him.

Shade on the other hand had thought that Jide had at least been fond enough of her to marry her and that love would come later, but to her dis- appointment he had carried on with his girlfriends and did not even bother to conceal the fact. The result had been that she began to lose interest in the home. She discovered that

Jide was even more conceited as a married man than as a single man and was constantly concerned about his attractiveness to women. Whenever they went out together, he would look longingly into the eyes of any pretty girl they passed as if forcing a recognition. When he did this, it was as if Shade did not exist. He would not even answer when she spoke to him.

This was because he did not bother to listen to her. It was humiliating for her, more so when she knew that she was not bad-looking herself. In desperation she had sought the advice of friends who had told her to pay more attention to herself and become the glamour girl she had been during her student days. That should make Jide sit up and notice, they reasoned. This she did, but to her surprise and amusement Jide did not take kindly to it at all. At home he would rave at her for having tried to be the life and soul of a party they had just attended. He called it behaving like a whore, and a cheap one at that. Never mind that she had caught him cuddling a girl in a corner at that same party.

As Evbu sat there watching Jide, she felt sorry that he was so unhappy. She was not quite sure whether she was still in love with him or if she was just flattered that he still wanted to stay and talk to her. She could see that his thoughts were far away and she had no doubt that they were of his wife.

'Jide,' she said gently after a while. 'You said you wanted to speak to me. What is it about?'

'Just to tell you, Evbu, that I still love you very much and would like us to continue from where we left off.'

'Are you joking?' exclaimed Evbu. 'You seem to forget that you are married.'

'I know, but as the marriage is now on the rocks, and heaven knows that I don't want to save it, why can't I let my heart rule and go with the only lady I have ever loved?'

"That's all nicely spoken, Jide, but just think for a moment. If your marriage had not hit the rocks you would not have thought of coming back to "the only lady you ever loved!" You must have thought that one up when you bumped into my friend and me just

now.'

'But you are quite wrong there. Ever since we parted I have kept track of your activities. I was told of the various men you dated. I was really worried when that chap Edegbe became quite serious about your relationship."

'Why? Didn't you think he was right for me?'

'It wasn't that. I just didn't want you to become too attached to him and eventually marry him. I know that I was stupid not to have married you in the first place, but I always knew that we would get back together at the end. I shall ask Shade to leave, and after some months you can move in with me and everything will be like before. Gosh, I can't wait to have you all to myself once more."

Evbu was not surprised to hear Jide talk in such a naive way. Once he had thought up something, he never saw any difficulty in the way. He always behaved as if problems were things you could wipe off a slate at will.

'How do you know that your wife will be willing to move out just because you tell her to? And what about your daughter? Will you just deprive her of her home at the drop of a hat like that? I can see you've not changed one bit. What about me? Am I willing to return to you? What sort of future do you offer?'

'I don't foresee any difficulty. Shade is too proud of a lady to stay in a house after she's been told she's not wanted.'

'Are you going to tell her she's not wanted?' 'Yes, why not? After all, she's hardly ever in the house. I love my daughter, but I don't intend to lead an unhappy life in order to give her a home. I'm sure she wouldn't be happy growing up in a home where there is no love.'

'Jide?'

'Yes, darling? You don't know how I have longed all these months to be able to call you my very own again, Evbu, my love.'

'Listen, Jide. Have you asked me if I still care for you?'

'Oh,' he said confidently, 'I know you still do. True love like the type we had for each other does not die that easily.'

'But I don't anymore,' she said quietly. Now that she had said it out, she was not quite sure herself if it was the truth. She knew however that her love for him was certainly dampened by the careless way he spoke about asking his wife and child to leave. True, she had longed for him all these months, the same way you long for something that is suddenly taken out of your reach, but she was not sure that she now wanted to spend the rest of her life with him.

Any girl married to Jide would never know peace. He was too conceited to be able to give a girl emotional security. He always believed that any girl he met could not help falling under his spell. Jide looked at her for a moment and then smiled. Of course, he told himself, Evbu had always played hard to get and this occasion was certainly not an exception. He would have to summon all his old charms and win her over.

This time it would have to be for good. He was not going to let her go again. If Shade agreed to give him a divorce later, he would marry Evbu and give up chasing after girls. He was, in fact, being truthful when he had said that he had been thinking of Evbu constantly. For months he had stalked her, and this afternoon had actually followed her to the hotel. It had taken a lot of courage though to break in on her friend and her as he was not sure how she would receive him.

'Evbu, darling,' he said earnestly, 'I know how you must feel. You must hate me very much for the uncivilised way I treated you, but please find it in your heart to forgive me a little each day. I know I'm asking for a lot, but I have always loved you and will still continue to do so if you let me. I have had many girls so far in my life but I know that none holds so much as a match to you. I was foolish to have let you go in the past and I don't need to tell you now that no single day passed without my thinking of you. Even while saying "I do" on my wedding day. I could not help wishing it was you at my side. I'm not ashamed to own up to all this.

Perhaps it was not fair to the girl I married, but there it is. I could not help my love for you and I still can't. Can you still remember that day, all those years ago, when we first met in Benin? Look me in the eye, Evbu, and tell me you don't love me anymore. That way, I will know that you are really speaking from your heart, and I will go away and never bother you again."

Evbu's eyes filled with tears. She knew that she still loved him despite the seeming

hopelessness of the case and the constant
heartache such love would always bring her.
She was confused and did not know what to
say. Jide came round to her side, wiped her
tears and took her arm.

'Darling, let's go for a quiet talk somewhere.
Shall we go to your place?'

Evbu nodded.

'Let's go in your car,' he said. 'I could
take a taxi back later to pick up mine.'

They drove quietly back to Evbu's flat, but once
inside, Jide could hardly wait to take her into
his arms.

'Darling, darling Evbu. You can't guess
how often I have wanted to do this over the past
two and a half years. I almost went mad with
desire for you. Each time I took a girl in my
arms, I tried to imagine it was you. It became a

regular game of mine. This time, thank God, you'll be mine for good. What a relief it will be to have you by my side. Say you still love me, darling. It's terribly important to me.'

'I guess I still love you, Jide, or we would not find ourselves like this. But is there a future for us together? I'm confused.'

'Don't be, my love, things will sort themselves out.'

'But promise me something, Jide.' 'What is it?'

"That you won't ask your wife and child to leave. It would seem as if I'm responsible for the break-up of your marriage.'

'But you're not. You have nothing to do with it.' "That's true, but that's not what people will think. They'll say that I did all in my power to get you back. I don't want that on my conscience.'

'Grow up, darling. You can't please everyone. People will always talk. Don't think of the future. Think of now. Of you and me and our love. Shall we go out or stay in? Or are you expecting a boyfriend?'

'Don't be silly, Jide. I thought you were well- informed about my dates. Let's stay in. I'm sure we have a lot to discuss.'

They talked and talked that evening about every- thing they could think of. Then at midnight, Jide had to leave.

'I wish I could stay on longer darling, but I have to go home and see Bola. Sometimes she won't go to bed until she has seen me. Shade said that she was attending a party in Ikeja.'

'When do I see you then?'

'I'm on duty all day tomorrow, so I shall see you on Monday evening.'"

'Alright. Here, let me drive you back to the hotel to pick up your car.'

"Thanks, darling, but I don't like the idea of you driving back alone so late at night."

'Nothing will happen to me. It's not far to go and this is a very busy area. Look, some shops are still open. To tell the truth I want to be with you a little longer.'

'Oh, my love, I do too. I'm almost tempted now to

stay the night with you.'

'Your little girl will be disappointed if she doesn't see any of you except the nanny when she wakes up

in the night.'

'You're quite right. Let's go then.'

When they got to the car park they clung to each other, kissing passionately. At last they let go and Jide got into his car.

'I'll see you back to your street and then go home." 'Won't that delay you further? I'm sure I'll be alright.'

'I won't come in. I will drive off as soon as I see the lights go up in your flat.'

'Alright then. I can't wait to see you on Monday evening.'

'Me too,' he said, and blew her a kiss. He drove behind her back to the house, saw the lights go up and drove off.

Evbu slept well that night. She felt happy about the reunion with Jide but at the same time had a sense of foreboding. Somehow, she just knew that they could never be husband and wife. After the affectionate way he had spoken of his daughter she did not see him cold heartedly sending her and the mother out of the home. All the same it had been good to feel Jide's lips on hers once again. She decided not to think of the future.

She lazied around all that day. The following day, Monday, she dressed with care and went to the office. As usual her boss, Mrs Niyi, was in early. 'Hello, Evbu,' she called through the connecting door. 'You're all dolled up. Any special date this afternoon?'

'No, Mrs Niyi,' laughed Evbu.

'Well, you look lovely and happy. That's good. It means you're ready to tackle the day's job. We have a busy day ahead of us.'

The morning soon slipped by. After lunch at the staff canteen, Evbu went back to her office to read the papers and while away the time until work began again at 1.30 p.m. At the back page of a local paper, she caught sight of the headline:

"DOCTORS LOSE IN THE FIGHT TO SAVE THE LIFE OF DR. J.J."

'A popular Lagos doctor, Dr. Jide Jones died yesterday afternoon as a result of the injuries he sustained in a car crash on Saturday night along the Carter Bridge. He ran headlong into a stationary lorry which had broken down and had been left in an unlit area of the ...

Evbu fell down unconscious. She regained consciousness after a few minutes and was taken home. Mrs Niyi sent along a girl from the office to stay with Evbu until a doctor from the firm's clinic arrived. He examined her and gave her some tablets, and recommended a few days' rest. When she felt better, Evbu sent her colleague off. Kemi called on her way home from work.

She had heard the news that morning but had been unable to contact Evbu. She was shocked to find Evbu looking so ill. She wondered why she should be so affected by the death of some- one who had jilted her so long ago. At worst, she had thought that Evbu would be sorry about the news. She decided not to leave her by herself in the flat. She went home to get a few clothes and then came back to spend three days with her. When Mrs Niyi called the next day to find out how

Evbu was, it was Kemi who explained everything to her. Mrs Niyi was sympathetic and said that Evbu should take a week off to recover.

To ease the shock, Kemi tried to get Evbu to talk about Jide.

'When did you last see him?' she asked.

'Last Saturday. I saw him briefly at the Harbour Hotel. It was the first time I had seen him since we broke up.'

'Really? Did you speak to him?'

'Yes, we greeted each other and asked about relations. That was all.'

Evbu did not mean to keep the truth from Kemi, but she knew how much she loved to spread news around. If she had told her that she, Evbu, was probably the last person Jide spoke to, and that they had been reconciled and spent some hours together before his crash, the news would be all over Lagos in no time.

It would not be fair to Shade to know in her grief that her husband had spent his last conscious hours in this world saying passionate things to his ex-girlfriend.

Although Evbu did not want to overdo the grief she felt for Jide, contrary to the advice Kemi had given her she could not keep away from the burial.

Was it curiosity on her part to see members of his family? She couldn't tell. She knew that she had to be there. At the church she had sat in an inconspicuous corner, and at the cemetery, after Shade and the others had moved off, she hurriedly went to the graveside and threw in some flowers and soil, just before the diggers filled in the pit. She lingered beside the grave thinking of those last few hours. Surprisingly, she was dry-eyed and could think clearly even though her heart was full of grief. Perhaps her reunion with Jide was not meant to be.

It was ironic that he should die just after he had decided that he wanted her more than anything else in the world. Such was the cruel hand of fate. She thought of that day they had met in Benin City for the first time all those years back. She tried feebly not to feel too much pity for Jide and herself over the life they might have had together. Instead she tried to think of the effect his death would have on his aged parents and his immediate family. Shade would eventually remarry, but what about little Bola? She was too young to understand anything and would never know how much her father loved her.

Evbu moved away from the now deserted graveyard and walked towards her car. She shivered slightly in the cool evening breeze. As she got into her car, a voice hailed her from behind.

'Excuse me, please, lady.'

Evbu turned and saw a man of about thirty or more striding towards her. He was tall and a bit on the hefty side. His accent suggested he was not Nigerian, or was an emigrant Nigerian. Must be American, decided Evbu, when he spoke again with a drawl.

'Sorry to bother you, lady. Did you come for the burial of Mr Jones?'

'Yes.'

'Are you his widow by any chance?' 'No.'

'I'm sorry if you feel I'm probing. You see, Jide and I were at King's College together about fourteen years ago. I left soon after my School Certificate for the United States and this is only my second visit since then. I arrived only yesterday and saw Jide's obituary and burial arrangements in the papers this morning. I see I'm too late to pay my last respects. Do you know how I can contact his family?'

'You could ask at the Teaching Hospital. I'm not related to the family. I was just an acquaintance of his.'

At this point, Evbu began to weep silently. It was true. She was nothing more than an acquaintance. Any attempt on her part to show the grief she really felt would be regarded as a 'put-on' by other people. 'Here lady,' said the man, offering his handkerchief. 'Is there a friend around who can see you home? You are obviously not in a condition to drive yourself home.

You could take a taxi, but that would mean leaving your car here, and it might be stolen.' "Thank you for your concern,' said Evbu quietly. 'I'm sorry to exhibit myself like I did. I'm sure I can drive if I pull myself together.'

'Well, if you're sure you'll be alright, then I'll take my leave of you. I want to go and offer my condolences to Jide's family.'

Evbu started the car, but her hands trembled violently on the steering wheel. She suddenly didn't want to be left alone. She looked up helplessly at the stranger.

'Could you drive me home, please?' She looked doubtful at him. It was not her habit to ask strange men to drive her home, but she was past caring now. She was exhausted and all she wanted to do was go home and lie down. If he turned out to be an armed robber or a kidnapper, well, God help her.

The man could guess what was going through her mind, and he smiled.

'I'll gladly drive you home, lady. Please move over, and tell me where you live. You'll have to direct me as I'm not used to all the one-ways and whatnots. By the way, my name is Steve Mayo, and I'm a Computer Engineer.'

'I'm Evbu Isibor. I work as a secretary.'

'Nice to know you. Somehow, your face looks familiar. Have we met before at a party or somewhere else?'

'I don't think so, although I must say your face looks vaguely familiar too.'

'Anyway, we'll talk about that some other time. Right now you need medical care. Do you have some aspirin at home or can I get you some at a drug- store?'

'I have some at home, thank you.'

When they got to where Evbu lived, Steve accompanied her to her flat and helped her on to the couch. 'Can I call in one of your neighbours? You should not be alone."

'Oh, I'll be alright shortly. I just feel weak and tired. I'll take some aspirins and go to bed. Thanks for bringing me home."

"That's alright. Well, I'll be on my way then,' he said, but he still stood there.

'I'm sorry I can't make you a cup of tea or something. I'm really tired."

'Just try and rest. If I can, I might pop in tomorrow to find out how you feel, and we will try and recall where we had met before.'

'Alright. See you then, and thank you.'
'Goodbye.'

'Goodbye.'

She then locked the door to her flat, took some aspirins and went straight to bed. She slept heavily and woke up very late the next day, a Sunday.

To take her mind off her grief, she kept herself busy that day, tidying the flat and doing her laundry. She did not even bother to change from her housecoat and she prayed that no one would call. She did not think she could face talking to anyone or making an attempt at being sociable.

If anyone rang the bell she would not reply, she decided. She hoped fervently that Steve, the stranger who had driven her home the day before, would not turn up. As it happened no one called, so she went to bed early so as to be in the office on time the next day.

Evbu made sure she kept herself busy both at home and in the office during the next few months. She withdrew completely from the social scene and did not date anyone. Everything seemed so futile to her as far as love was concerned. She was unlucky in love, she decided. Perhaps there was a jinx on her. How else could she explain her ill-luck? Both her younger sisters were engaged to be married.

She, at twenty-eight, had no marriage in sight. She did not lack suitors but she refused to have just anyone for a husband. It would have to be someone she cared deeply for, and who also cared for her. It would be terrible getting married to someone she did not love just so that she would not die a spinster. She believed so much in love in a marriage. It was what had bound her parents together and she knew that, despite the fact that her father had been a poor man who had a fiery temper, her mother had been quite happy with him and had struggled by his side. His death had completely shattered her and she had not looked at any other man since, although she was still an attractive woman in her early fifties.

Sometimes, however, Evbu frequently. Sometimes, wondered if she was not being too fussy about her choice of husband. Someone like Kemi would have made the best of the situation and settled down. Marriage to Edegbe might have turned out well, after all. He had worshiped her and she had been fond of him.

Chapter 7

Six months after Jide's death, Evbu had a phone call at the office.

'Is that Miss Isibor?'

'Yes, who is speaking, please?'

'I'm sure you won't remember me. I'm Steve Mayo.'

'Steve Mayo. I er . . . er...'

'I was the guy who drove you home from Ikoyi cemetery on the..."

'Oh, yes. Yes! Thank you ever so much for your kind gesture. I'm sorry I was such a nuisance that day.'

'You weren't. You needed help and I was on hand to give it, so there!'

'All the same, it was kind of you to help a total stranger.'

'Not at all. You remember I told you that your face looked familiar? Well, I got thinking, and it all came back to me.'

'Oh?'

'Yes. Cast your mind back. A painful subject though. Anyway, several years ago you were at a restaurant with Jide and a guy came behind him and put his hands over Jide's eyes and prevented him from turning around, and you were asked to describe this guy."

'Oh, oh, I remember now. It was at the "Chic Restaurant". It all comes back to me now. Jide had just gained admission into LUTH to do his course and we were out celebrating.'

"We were not introduced but I will never forget a face I've seen.'

'But you did not sound American that day. I mean there was no drawl. Did you say that you were at King's College with Jide?'

'Sure! My father was out here on attachment to a company so Jamie, my brother, and I were at King's College for about two years.'

'I see.'

'Look, can I come over and see you this evening?' 'Er, I don't know, er,' began Evbu. 'What for, anyway?'

'Oh, it's alright if you are not free. I only wanted to come and explain why I was not able to turn up that day to find out how you were, like I had promised to do the evening I drove you home. I felt guilty not checking you up since no one else knew how ill you were. I thought it was more polite explaining to you face to face, but not to worry..

'Oh, no,' Evbu broke in. 'I'm sorry I was a bit brusque just now. It's unpardonable of me. Please come. I'm not going out. When would you like to call?'

'At about seven. Are you sure you don't mind?'
'Now, now, Steve. May I call you Steve?'

'Yes, lady, you can.

'Now, Steve, I shall expect you at seven this evening.'

'Okay. See you then."

"The address is..."

'Not to worry. I remember the place, or have you moved since?'

'No. I'm still at the same house.'

'Fine. Goodbye.'

'Goodbye. I shall expect you."

After putting the phone down, Evbu felt ashamed of herself for having been a bit rude to Steve. She could not say what had come over her. Why hadn't she wanted to see him? She seemed to be shying away from contact with any man.

The man was only being polite and nice and there she was behaving as if he was trying to date her. Why should he bother about her? If he had wanted a date, there were lots of prettier and younger girls in town he could ask out.

Why else did he want to see her but for the reason he had stated? She would have to check this impulse of hers of jumping to the wrong conclusions, or she would lose friends.

To make amends she decided she would give Steve dinner. If he was going to call at seven he would not have had dinner yet.

She prepared some jollof rice, fried ripe plantains and stew, then she tidied up her sitting room and put on a simple dress and light make-up. She could not be bothered to dress to impress, so long as what she had on was clean. She wished he would hurry up, though, so that she could finish off the interesting novel she was reading before going to sleep.

When Steve had not turned up by eight-thirty, Evbu decided to have her supper and coil up with her book. Perhaps it would be like last time and he would not turn to delay having her meal any longer. As she was at all, so there was no need for her to dish out her food in the kitchen, the doorbell rang. She went to answer it.

'Good evening, Miss Isibor,' said Steve breathlessly. 'I'm terribly sorry I'm late. The traffic jam from the mainland was unbelievable. I thought I'd never get here.'

'What a shame,' said Evbu. 'Please come in and sit down, Steve.'

"Thanks, lady. May I call you by your first name?' 'Of course! It's Evbu.' 'Ev-bu.'

'Evbu. You sort of glide over the 'v' and the 'b'. Evbu.'

'Evbu.'

"That's it. You pronounce it like a native.'

'Oh, I'm sure you're flattering me, although I must say that I'm pretty good at pronouncing Nigerian names.'

Steve looked at Evbu curiously. She was quite different from the grief-stricken woman he had helped some months before. He had not realised how tall and attractive she was. She looked much younger than he had supposed- probably it was the garb she had on the last time he had seen her. What graceful carriage she had too!

'I said what would you like to drink?' said Evbu, laughing. 'You seem miles away."

'Pardon me, Evbu. I was not miles away. I was only admiring your lovely flat. I will have a coke, please.'

"That's just what I don't have. What about a beer?'

'Okay, half a bottle will do, thanks."

'I made some dinner. I thought you wouldn't have had time for some before coming."

"That's great! I'm starving! I had resigned myself to having snacks when I got back to my hotel tonight.'

"At which hotel are you staying?" "The Grove."

'Is it comfortable?'

'Quite. And the service is not bad-clean linen. polite waiters, and fairly good food. This is my second time there.'

'Oh, you're not based here then?'

'No. This is delicious!' he said as they began to eat. "Thank you."

'No, I'm not based here. I'm a Computer Engineer with a firm in New York. Members of our staff are sent out here from time to time to assist in a training programme in the various parts of the country where our computers have been installed.'

'Are you sent each time?'

'No, not necessarily. This is my second time, though, and I think it's because I've lived in this country before that I've been put on this assignment for two years. We come in a team of two."

'You like it then?'

'Very much. We come every six months, and we stay for two or three weeks.'

'How often do you run into your old schoolmates?' 'Pretty often. Do you know that KC boys are to be found in most top positions?'

'Hm! Don't you think you're a bit biased?' 'Maybe. But everyone I've come across is doing well.'

"That speaks well for the school. Have some more dodo.'

'No, thank you. I'm very full already. You cook well and I've enjoyed the food so much that I'm afraid I've overeaten.'

'Oh, that's alright. You'll be able to sleep soundly.'

'I hope so. Here, let's clear up together.' "Thank you."

They did the dishes together and afterwards relaxed in the sitting room drinking some wine and chatting.

Steve told her about his family. There were his parents, his brother Jamie, who was a doctor, himself, and Debbie who was a teacher. They all lived in New York. His father had retired from his firm and now spent most of his time writing poems, and his mother was very much involved in church work. He, Steve, lived in a flat of his own and was not yet married, although he had several girlfriends, the special one being Kate, who ran a beauty salon. Both his brother and sister were married with two children each. He enjoyed his job and was not ready to settle down just yet.

'And now, it's your turn to tell me about yourself.' "There isn't much to say,' she began nervously. 'Well, say what little there is.'

She told him about her parents, brothers and sisters, and then a little bit about her childhood in Isi and Benin City.

'May I ask you a pointed question if you don't mind?' he asked her when she had finished.

'Go on,' she said, smiling. 'I can guess what it is, though.'

'What then?' he asked laughing.

'My relationship with Jide, isn't it?'

'Precisely. Just curiosity on my part. You don't have to answer if it's too painful a subject. You were so overwhelmed by his death.'

'Yes, I was,' said Evbu slowly. 'I don't mind talking about it. In fact, I think it would help me to come to terms with myself."

Slowly, she explained how she and Jide had first met in Benin City and how their relationship had developed, and then the years of closeness which followed and the break up. She made no mention of the reason for the break up or the reconciliation later.

'Hm, very interesting,' he said, 'although there are obvious gaps I guess you don't want to fill in.' 'Not for a stranger, at any rate,' she laughed. 'Of course not. How discreet you are! Well, I must go now, it's getting late,' he added and got up.

'You've not explained why you did not call the day after we last met,' said Evbu.

'Oh, thanks for reminding me. Your delicious food made me forget. Actually, I went with a friend to Ibadan early the next morning and we came back quite late at night. The following day, Monday, I had to fly back to

New York. I was worried about you all alone and thought it was silly of me not to have notified a neighbour about your condition so that an eye could be kept on you.'

'Steve, I'm terribly grateful for what you did and I'm particularly flattered by your concern."

'I like helping wherever I can, Evbu. Well, thanks for the lovely meal and for your company. I've en- joyed myself. I'll ring you tomorrow. Goodnight.'

'Goodnight.'

Evbu did not pick up her book as soon as Steve left, as she had intended. Instead she sat for some time musing over his visit. She had felt very much at ease and relaxed with him, and she had enjoyed their chat. She was usually very reserved with strangers, but there was something in Steve which seemed to draw her

out of herself. He looked so solid and reliable-
the type you could confide in. A good friend.

It was mostly curiosity which had made
Steve get in touch again with Evbu, although he
had actually been worried that first night about
her, and had wanted to apologise for not
checking up on her condition the next day. He
had thought that it was more polite to apologise
face to face rather than on the phone. He had
been surprised that evening at the
transformation in Evbu-instead of the haggard
looking dame with tear-stained face, whose
hands trembled on the wheel of her car, he had
found a cool and attractive lady. The only thing
that still linked the two was the little sadness
one could detect in her eyes when she spoke of
Jide.

They must have been very much in love.
Now he could understand why she had not
wanted him to call on her. She seemed to be

shying away from people, trying to live in a shell.

He had enjoyed her company that night and he could tell that she had also enjoyed his. She was a good listener and had a sense of humour which matched his own. He had found her very attractive and desirable, and had had to control the strong impulse he had had, while they had been standing close together in the kitchen, to take her in his arms. He was glad that he had mastered his feelings.

It would have frightened her and she would have scurried back into her shell. She must be allowed to thaw gradually. He would like to see her happy once more. 'Hey man!' Steve admonished himself. 'Just what are you thinking of doing? You've not fallen for her, have you? Or are you just sorry for her? What about Kate back home?'

Steve knew that he did not fall for girls easily, and that he was definitely not sorry for Evbu.

To salve his conscience that night, he sat down and wrote Kate a long and an affectionate letter telling her how much he missed her. She was one of his current girlfriends, and although they were not engaged, they got on very well. She was sensational in every way and he was fond of her. He missed her a lot. He thought of Kate-her shapely figure, her wriggly walk and the way she arched an eyebrow when she disapproved of anything.

She was quite popular in their social circle and he was proud of her. She had made a success of her beauty parlour. Steve was a bit worried, however, when thoughts of Evbu kept intruding while he was thinking of Kate. What was happening to him, he wondered? Well, the best thing was not to see Evbu again.

For courtesy sake he would ring her up and thank her for the dinner she had given him, and that would be that. He was in Nigeria to work, and work he must. He must not get involved in any affair of the heart. But, two days later, he rang Evbu up to thank her for the dinner. She seemed delighted to hear from him and they got chatting.

When Steve put down the phone, he was horrified to realise that he had asked her out that evening. He could not say what had made him do it.

This time Evbu took extra care with dressing up for her date. 'It's certainly no love match,' she told herself, 'but if I'm coming out of social seclusion, then I'd better do so with a bang. It wouldn't do to run into old friends looking like a hag.'

Remembering that American girls usually like jeans and such like, she decided to go with an African-a tightfitting skirt in blue and white adire and a matching headtie. She put on large hoop earrings, white shoes and carried a white handbag. As usual, she used light make-up. The overall effect was stunning and she liked what she saw in the mirror.

'I hope he won't think me a tart in all these tight- fitting clothes,' she thought, a little belatedly, as the doorbell went.

'Hello, Steve,' she said on opening the door.

'Hello, Evbu,' he replied, and whistled under his breath as he admired her, although he made no com- ment. Evbu was pleased at his reaction, but was a bit disappointed that he had not been more demonstrative. She thought fleetingly of what Jide's reaction would have been, and she felt the tiniest pang of pain. She decided to comment on Steve's outfit.

'I see you've gone Nigerian this evening. That's a lovely embroidered jumper you've got on. Did you buy it here?'

"Thanks. Yes, I bought it at the Kingsway Stores, but I'm having some made by a local tailor that a friend recommended. These things are quite popular back home, too."

'Oh yes? Would you like to have a drink before we go out?'

'No, thank you. If you're ready, let's start.'

'Right.'

They had drinks and then dinner at the Harbour Hotel. It was the first time Evbu had gone there since the afternoon Jide had had a talk with her there about reconciliation. Her eyes clouded over for a fraction of a second when she and Steve strolled through the garden.

After dinner, they drove around in Steve's rented car for a while and then parked and strolled along the well-lit Marina. They sat down under a coconut tree and admired the ships on the lagoon, and the villages which lay beyond whose distant lights they could see. It all looked romantic and Evbu sighed contentedly while throwing pebbles into the water. Once she glanced sideways at Steve, and found him looking at her curiously.

'Why are you looking at me like that?' she asked him.

'I was trying to compose a poem about you in this atmosphere.'

'Really? Let's hear it then.'

'No, not now. Maybe one day. I don't want to spoil the magic.'

Evbu's heart missed a beat. What did he mean by that? It was nice being with Steve. She felt like laying her head on his broad shoulder, but she knew that it wouldn't do. He had made no move to touch her-not even to take her hand.

She wondered what he thought of her. He certainly was not generous with his compliments. In fact he had paid her none so far. Quite different from her notions of Americans-always 'babying' and 'darlinging' one. When they got back to her flat Evbu invited him for coffee but he declined.

'No, baby. Thanks all the same. You look tired. I'll walk you to your door.

'Oh, no need for that, Steve,' said Evbu, a little hurt that he had refused her offer of coffee.

'Politeness demands it,' said Steve gently. 'Alright, then. Before you go I must say that I've enjoyed myself very much this evening. To be can- did, I've not had such a lovely time for some time. Thank you, Steve.'

'You're welcome, Evbu. I'm flattered, and I've en- joyed being with you too.' Evbu waited to hear more, but nothing was forthcoming.

When they got to the door of her flat, they stood facing each other and Steve made as if to take her in his arms, but he checked himself, gave her a peck on the cheek, murmured 'Goodnight' and dashed down the steps.

Evbu sighed and went into her flat thoughtfully. What was happening? Steve behaved one minute as if he wanted her and the next as if he had found her repulsive.

She was baffled. She had never experienced such drama before. Not every man she met fell for her, but those who took her out usually made it plain that they found her attractive and they showered their compliments.

Steve was a different kettle of fish. Could it be that he did not find her as sophisticated as his girls back home? Was she too old-fashioned and conservative in her ways? What was she worried about anyway? She was not in love with him? What did it matter whether he found her attractive or not. She was just being vain.

When Steve was in bed that night, he thought about Evbu, and found himself getting angry with himself. He had behaved like an immature fool! He was drawn to Evbu and wanted her, but a part of him also wanted to keep away. They had been together just twice. Was that sufficient to make him want her like he knew he did? He was not usually so silly about girls. Did he come all the way from New York, where there were lots of real hot mamas, to get involved with a Nigerian girl, granted one as charming as Evbu?

He was behaving in a fashion alien to him. He was not usually so tongue tied with girls. In fact, on the contrary, he never hid his admiration of any dame, and this used to make his girlfriends sulk. What did he want from Evbu? He could not say. Well, he must stop seeing her, he decided firmly. But why? He could just have a fling and then go back to Kate. There was no law which said that he could not have a casual affair out here, he tried to convince himself, but in his heart he knew he could not do that with Evbu. He would not want to-rather he would like to take her, keep her and cherish her all his life.

Hey! What's this? He leapt out of bed and doused his head with cold water to make him come back to his senses. Eventually, Steve's confusion exhausted him and he fell into a restless sleep. Evbu rang him up two days later to thank him for the lovely time she had had. He was very guarded in his short conversation with her this time. He did not want to discover at the end that he had asked her out again without meaning to. Evbu was surprised that Steve sounded so subdued on the phone. She was further surprised when he made no mention of seeing her again.

During the days that followed, there was no word from him.

'Well, that's that, then!' she thought. The friend- ship died without even taking-off. She was not going to call on him. She had her pride! Could he, however, have discovered something he did not like about her? It would be nice to know-not that it mattered in the least.

He had told her on their last date when he would leave for New York, so when she did not hear from him again, she phoned his hotel and made discreet inquiries. She was told that he had indeed left.

She drifted on during the following months. Thoughts of Jide were now few and far between. She heard that Shade had had another baby. It was a boy and she had called him 'Jide'. Evbu was surprised that she did not feel jealous about it, as she had done when they had Bola. In a way, she was glad that there was someone to carry Jide's name for- ward, whatever that meant. She felt relieved-as if a burden had been lifted off her shoulders. She did not see any point in grieving over Jide anymore. There was a wife, a daughter and now a son to continue to do that for him.

She continued working hard in the office but went back to her social seclusion. It was only Kemi she visited occasionally. Kemi had remarried and was expecting a baby. Although they still were fond of each other, they had less in common to talk about now, as Kemi was very excited about her pregnancy and would hardly discuss anything else. Although Evbu was glad to see Kemi so happy, she could not help feeling bored and worn-out by it all.

It was a relief when the baby boy finally arrived and Kemi went to nurse him in Abeokuta where her mother could help. Evbu was the godmother when the baby was christened. She played her role well on the day, and no one could guess how heavy her heart was. Even Kemi was too busy in her new role to discern the unhappiness in her friend.

Gradually through the following months, Evbu lost weight and became careless with her appearance. She thought of Steve a lot and kept going over their last outing together, trying to find out where she had stepped out of line.

One day, Mrs Niyi called her into her office at the end of the day.

'Sit down, please Evbu,' she said.

"Thank you, Mrs Niyi.'

'Is there anything wrong, Evbu. I'm sorry if I'm probing, but I'm full of concern for you. Over the months I've watched you get worse both in your appearance and in your work. You don't look happy any more. Are you still grieving over your ex- boyfriend who died so long ago?'

'No,' said Evbu slowly.

'What is it then?' Mrs Niyi asked gently. 'You've completely changed. Tell me. I might be able to help. Is it a money problem?'

'No, madam. It's just that I'm not happy. I can't really say why. Nothing seems to matter anymore." And she burst out crying. Mrs Niyi prudently allowed her to calm down before asking further questions.

'Has it anything to do with your not being married?' she asked when Evbu had at last managed to calm down.

'I don't think so,' she said sniffing. 'I've not worried about it although I naturally think it would be nice to settle down. I know it will come.'

'Hm! Who are you going out with at the moment?

I don't mean his name, I mean is he someone you are quite fond of?'

'Actually, I've not been out on a date for about eight months or more. So there's really no one.'

'Why?' asked Mrs Niyi, surprised.

'Oh, I just... just got fed up. It all seemed so futile. Nothing ever came out of these relationships. for I always have one thing or the other against men that want to marry me. It's either that, or they end up not wanting to marry me either.'

'Well, that's life. I think, though, that something must have happened consciously or unconsciously to make you become anti-men and unsociable."

'I don't think I'm anti-men as such, madam. Actually, there was Steve Mayo, an American who..."

'Ah, let's hear about him, then."'

So, Evbu told her everything that had taken place between them.

'Are you fond of him,' asked Mrs Niyi when Evbu had stopped talking, 'or are you hurt because he dropped you suddenly?'

'Er, madam, I cannot really say fairly that he dropped me since he never actually took up with me. It was not love at first sight but I had a feeling that something was about to develop between us, on my part as well as, I thought, his part. But he just suddenly stopped seeing me. He could not get away fast enough. I felt humiliated. It was as if there was something nasty about me that he had just discovered.'

'Why didn't you contact him after that?'

'I did. I rang him up to thank him for a lovely evening, but his conversation was guarded-which was unlike him-and he did not express a wish to see me again. I was too proud to contact him myself after this. Oh, I don't know.'

'Has he been to the country since?'

'He must have been, for he had told me that he comes every six months. I did not find out, however.'

'Hm! I don't know what advice to give you. If he were in the country, I would have said that you should get in touch with him and invite him to your place. On seeing him again you would have known whether you're actually in love with him. It does happen you know-you see a man you've been hankering after and you ask yourself what you ever saw in him. But at least it will help get him out of your mind, if that's what you want. The other thing to do is to shake yourself up and become more active. Take an interest in your appearance and become more sociable.

That does not necessarily involve dating men if you don't want to. Getting married and settling down is great, but it is not an end in itself. If it comes your way and you're happy, that's good. If it doesn't right now, it will later. Meanwhile, show yourself worthy of being alive. You could take up a hobby-swimming, tennis, squash, badminton, what have you.

Anyway, develop an interest in something. It will give you a new lease of life. And now, about your work. The report you typed for me this morning was so bad that I decided I must have a serious talk with you to find out what exactly was wrong. See for yourself," she added, tossing the report into the 'Out' tray. 'I've never had to make one-twentieth as many corrections in any work you've done for me so far.'

Evbu took the report and gasped. It did not look like her work at all. The layout was terrible and there were lots of mistakes and overtyping.

'I'm terribly sorry, Mrs Niyi,' she said at length, her eyes beginning to cloud over once more. 'May I stay in and do it all over again?'

'No need for that, Evbu. Tomorrow morning will do. All I want you to do is to be happy again. I want the old sparkle back in your eyes. Life is short, so enjoy what you can of it while you can. Good luck and goodnight.'

'Goodnight, Mrs Niyi. Thanks for taking an interest in my affairs."

That night, Evbu thought over all her boss had told her that evening. She had not realised she had been slipping in her general demeanour.

She thought hard. She still wore trendy trendy outfits-Nigerian or foreign, yes, but sometimes not quite clean or ironed, hair not well-groomed, cracked fingernails, shoes not cleaned, etc... She recalled that a male acquaintance of hers had given her a quizzical look at a petrol station and had asked if she had been feeling alright. She had thought then that it was perhaps that she had looked and felt tired. She could not understand her own behaviour.

How could she go to pieces over Steve whom she hardly knew? When Jide had left her, she had not behaved like this. She had been hurt alright, but did not lose the zest for life. Funny! She must take a grip on herself. First and foremost, she decided she must take a holiday. Mrs Niyi granted her two weeks of her annual holiday. She went to Benin City to see her mother, but she moped around all day and did not enjoy her stay.

After four days, she had had enough, so on impulse she bought an air ticket for Kano. Evbu had never been to the northern parts of Nigeria although she had often had the urge to do so. She knew no one there and she had not thought she could afford the airfare and the hotel accommodation, but found that she had saved enough money, so there was nothing to prevent her from going there.

She hesitated at the thought of staying at a hotel, since it was not a widespread practice for ladies to lodge singly in hotels. After giving it some thought, she decided to brave it. After all it was the way she presented herself that people would judge her by. She was going there for a holiday and that was all.

Right from the airport, she found Kano a fascinating place. She was seeing the savannah area for the first time and she thought it was fabulous. Her hotel room was comfortable and she knew she was going to enjoy her stay. She intended to do lots of sightseeing because she had heard so much about the sights of Kano City. She would also buy lots of leather goods and other souvenirs to give to friends. Already, the girl at the reception had given her a tour guide which she had read avidly as soon as she had settled in her room. She was not going to allow herself a dull moment.

She was elated later that evening when, while taking a pre-dinner walk through the hotel grounds, she got catcalls from some workers nearby. Some of her usual confidence returned and she was in a good mood when she entered the restaurant for her meal. A waiter handed her a menu as soon as she was seated at an empty table. She was studying it when someone sat at her table and said, 'Hello, Miss Isibor.' When Evbu looked up and saw Steve Mayo, she almost jumped out of her skin.

'Steve, wherever did you spring from?" she asked when she could talk.

'Sshh, not so loud,' he said, smiling, and coming to her side of the table. 'Let's go and talk outside."

They went and sat at a table in the garden. Steve ordered drinks.

'Now, Evbu, you tell me what you are doing here.'" 'You haven't answered my question, Steve.' 'Ladies first."

'Oh, alright. I came here for a holiday and I'm staying at this hotel. I arrived this afternoon.'

'I see. Well, I'm here on business for a week and I arrived last night. But tell me. Why are you holidaying so far away from Benin City? Do you have relations here?'

'No, I don't. I've never been this way before but a friend who had been here, spoke highly of it so I decided to come.'

'I didn't know you were that adventurous. I had the impression that you were too conservative and well-protected.'

'When did you arrive in the country, Steve?' 'A week ago."

'I see,' said Evbu, with a quiet smile. 'What do you see?'

'Nothing. I see, that's all.'

'Are you angry with me, Evbu?'

'Any reason why I should be? And does it matter?'

'Yes, it matters a lot to me. Shall I tell you something, Evbu?'

'Please do.'

'I love you,' he said quietly, taking her hand across the table. 'I love you, Evbu.'

'You... you what? What did you say, Steve?' 'I said I love you. You look surprised."

'I am surprised. You avoided me after our evening out together, and you've been in the country for a week and have not thought fit to contact me and then out of the blue you tell me that you love me. What am I supposed to think?'

'It's true that I avoided you before I left last time, but I was at your place some days ago and a neighbour told me that you had gone travelling. I slipped a note under your door telling you that I was in the country and would like to see you urgently. You can check when you get back to Lagos.'

'Oh, I'm sorry, Steve, I always say the wrong things. Forgive me.'

'You're forgiven, baby. Let's go for a drive. I have lots of things to tell you.'

Evbu got up unsteadily. She could not quite make out what was happening. Steve turned up out of the blue; Steve declaring that he loved her. She just could not take it all in.

They drove around for a while in an exclusive residential area chatting about this and that. Then Steve parked under a tree by the side of a road. Gently he took Evbu into his arms and kissed her. Later, still with his arms around her, Steve asked, 'Do you still doubt if I love you, Evbu?'

'I can't say I doubt what you said, but could you please explain why you avoided me?'

'I was merely fighting against falling in love with you.'

'But why?'

'You see, you had seemed drained of life at Jide's death, and I'm sure you must have loved him very much. Some months later when we met again, you seemed to be retiring from people and not wanting to be disturbed.

When we went out together, you were more relaxed and you seemed to enjoy my company, but I did not want to force myself on you. I did not want to be the one who took Jide's place-who sort of caught you on the rebound. What puzzled me most was why you were so affected by his death when he had jilted you and married another girl several years before. To me it meant that you will continue to grieve all your life for him. I wouldn't want a girlfriend to keep on comparing me with another man. Then there was Kate, my girlfriend. I did not think it would be nice cheating on her here. But much as I tried to forget you, I couldn't. You were constantly on my mind all these months, and at last I had to admit that I was in love with you. I told Kate about it. Apparently, she had noticed a change in me so she was not surprised. She said I was silly not to have found out what you felt about me.'

'Really? You mean she did not mind your being in love with another girl?"

'Oh, Kate is great. You will like her. She is level- headed and cool. We are the best of friends. Actually, she is so much involved in business that she will not settle down for years yet. So, bless her, I suppose she does not want to play "the dog in the manger." We still go out every now and again. Now, Evbu, what do you think of me?'

"I think you're nice and kind and proud and unfair and lots of other things."

'Unfair, me?'

'Yes, Steve,' said Evbu, laughing and kissing him. 'You spring too many surprises.'

'How do you feel about me?'

'I love you, Steve.'

'Are you quite sure? You are not saying that out of sympathy?'

'Why should I? You can't guess what I've been through these past eight or nine months when I thought that I'd never see you again."

'Oh, don't I, baby?' he said, drawing her close. 'I had a very trying time myself. I had to decide what it was I really wanted.'

During the days that followed, Evbu found Steve a very kind and considerate person. He put others first and would go out of his way to please people, even those who were total strangers to him. She was amazed at the ease with which he could talk with people he had never met before.

She wondered what his minuses were, for nobody was perfect; and she also wondered where their relationship would take them. Experience had taught her to allow the future to take care of itself. She was not going to build up any dreams but would try and take whatever happened in her stride.

One thing she was quite sure of was that she was in love with Steve. Oh, not the heart-thumping love she had had for Jide, all burning and feverish. What she felt for Steve was a type of love that was calm and secure, and which filled her with a glow each time she saw him or thought of him. She felt as if he was an extension of herself.

Very shortly, Evbu's week was up and Steve put her on the plane for Lagos with the promise that he would arrive two days later.

Evbu went back to Lagos in a cloud of happiness. Mrs Niyi remarked on her cheerfulness on her first morning back at the office.

'Goodness, Evbu, there's no need for me to ask if you enjoyed your holiday. You're glowing! What happened to you?'

'I'm so happy I could dance, Mrs Niyi,' replied Evbu, and told her all that had happened.

'I'm glad for you, Evbu. I really am. I can see that I may soon start looking for another secretary.'

'Not so fast, madam. He has not asked me to marry him yet. I'm prepared to wait, though. I simply enjoy being with him. You can't imagine how nice he is. He is so good to me."

"That's lovely, Evbu. There's nothing like kindness in an association. Bring him to dinner at my place, let's see now, er, on Friday next week. Will he still be around then?'

'Yes. He has two more weeks before he goes back." 'So, shall we say 7.30pm next

Friday?' 'Yes, please, Mrs Niyi. That would be nice. Thank you very much.'

'Oh, that's alright, Evbu. I'll look forward to meeting him.'

When Steve got back to Lagos, he and Evbu spent most of their free time together. Evbu introduced him to Kemi, who was now back in Lagos with her baby and was once again involved in full-scale business. Her husband had bought her a van with which she supplied goods to various firms. Evbu could see that Kemi had matured considerably.

Kemi was a bit apprehensive about Evbu's relationship with Steve.

'Do you think he is right for you, Evbu?' 'Why? In what way?'

'I mean, he is a foreigner, isn't he? If you marry him, it means you will have to go with him to

New York. Will you like that? Won't it break your mother's heart to see you living so far away?'

'Kemi, Steve has not asked me to marry him yet, but I'm prepared to follow him to the end of the world if he does."

'Evbu,' laughed. Kemi, 'you always are stubborn when in love. I believe it's all those romantic novels you read where people fall in love and live happily ever after. You've got to be realistic, you know. New York is not Ibadan or Benin City or even Kano. It's very far away and it takes time for letters to get there or from there. I am not trying to dissuade you from whatever decision you're likely to take, but I only want you to look at your relationship from another angle.'

'I'm grateful for your concern for me, Kemi. You've been a good friend to me. I know I'm stubborn while in love, but I've matured a lot since Jide, and I now know precisely what I want out of life. I want love and happiness. I think I will find it with Steve. I love him and I know he loves me. If he wants me to marry him, I will not hesitate at all, but I have ceased to hanker after getting married. I only want to be happy. I have decided to join some charity organisations and do voluntary work for handicapped children at weekends. That way, I will be making other people happy as well.'

'My, my, Evbu. There are many sides to you. What does Steve think of all this?'

'He is very much for it. Apparently, his mother and his sister are involved in this type of work back in New York. In fact all members of his family are involved in one charity work or the other.'

'Well, I must say that's nice. I must give it a thought myself. I'll probably do something when my baby is older.'

The dinner with Mr and Mrs Niyi was a success. Evbu could see at once that Mrs Niyi liked Steve and thought he was right for her. Steve was polite and had elegant manners and Evbu was proud of him.

Steve went back to New York two days after the dinner at Mrs Niyi's, with a promise to write to Evbu as many times as he could manage. This time, Evbu got his address, for she intended to write to him even if he did not write first. But she did not need to worry. He wrote regularly once a week. His letters were passionate ones and Evbu replied in the same vein. He told her that he had spoken to his parents about their relationship. He also talked about his job. His assignment in Nigeria was coming to an end because the contract for training was about to expire.

He and his colleague had just two more trips to make to Nigeria and he had been told that he was likely to be sent to California the following year. Evbu did not know what to think or say. Did it mean that after two more visits it would all be over between her and Steve? Perhaps she could save up for a trip to New York. It would be nice to meet Steve's family and Kate. He had told her so much about them that it was as if she already knew them.

One Saturday afternoon, Evbu was cleaning out her flat when the doorbell went. 'Oh, brother! Someone would turn up just when I'm knee deep in dusting and polish,' she muttered to herself as she peered in the mirror and wiped her face. She opened the door with a jerk, prepared to dispose of whoever it was in seconds and get back to her job, but there on her doorstep was Steve grinning broadly.

'Goodness, Steve!' she exclaimed as he gathered her up in his arms. 'You will make me have heart failure one of these days. When did you arrive in Lagos?'

"This morning. I dumped my suitcase at my hotel and here I am.

'Oh, Steve,' she said, kissing him, 'it's wonderful to see you again.'

'You can't guess how much I've missed you, baby.'

'Sit down Steve. I'm sorry the whole place is topsy-turvy. It's my cleaning day. Was I mad when the doorbell went! Here, have a pouf and put up your feet while I quickly put this place in order, and then make lunch for us.'

"There goes the busy housewife. I'll do as you say and just sit and watch. I do feel a bit tired. The trip was quite sudden. We were told of it only a few days ago, and we had to rush around getting materials and the spare parts we would need."

'Oh, it's not the usual trip, then? Isn't it six months since you last came over?'

'It is more than six months, I think, but we were not due to come until next month. Something crop- ped up which required some parts and our immediate attention, so everything was combined.'

'Oh, I see. What food shall I make you? I have most things at home.'

"That's great. Light Amala and Okro, then. I just love it. Can I come and help?'

'No. You just rest. It will be ready in no time."
He dozed off in the chair and had to be woken
up by Evbu when she had set the food on the
table.

After lunch they lazed around and played
records. In the evening they decided to dine out.
First, Steve had to go to his hotel and change
his clothes.

When Steve came for her, Evbu was surprised
to see him looking a bit stern. 'What is it, Steve?
Why are you looking so serious?'

'I'm alright,' he said mysteriously, kissing her on
the lips. 'Come, Evbu, sit on my lap.'

Evbu sat on his lap, wondering what was
happening.

'Do you love me, Evbu?' he asked softly.

'What a silly thing to ask. Is that why
you're looking so serious? Of course I love you,

darling,' she said laughing, and kissing him on the nose.

'Will you marry me, Evbu?'

'   What?' she exclaimed, jumping up. She was totally unprepared for this.

'Will you marry me?' repeated Steve seriously, after pulling her to him again. Evbu's heart began to thump. It would be so easy to say 'yes' for she loved him, but what about her past? Should she tell him or should she not? There was no one to turn to for advice.

'Evbu, what's the matter? Why do you hesitate so long and why is your heart beating so fast? You do love me, don't you?'

'I love you with all my heart, Steve, but there is something you ought to know about me. Not pleasant at all. But I'd rather tell you about it now than have you find out later.'

'I see. What is it? Evbu?'

So Evbu told him about her 'career' in the nightclubs; her relationship with Pete and the cause of her quarrel with Jide; then she told him how she and Jide had been reconciled just before his accident. When she had finished, she could not look him in the face. She sat as far away from him as possible on the settee. When he did not say anything for some time, she stole a glance at his face.

'Well, Evbu,' he said at length trying to keep a straight face, but he couldn't and he burst out laughing.

'What's funny, Steve?' Evbu asked. "To me it's a serious matter."

'I'm sorry, love, but you should have seen your face when you were telling your story. It was as if you were confessing to a hideous crime.'

"That's what it is to me.'

"Then, my love, you've been too well-protected all your life. I can assure you that even a High School kid back home would have a more impressive story than yours to tell. What about me? If I told you half the things I'd been up to in my younger days, it would make you shudder. But my pride is that I was able to come out of it all unscathed. It was all part of growing up and my parents were very patient and tolerant about it. Don't you read foreign papers? Don't you wonder at the things which take place in the so-called civilised countries of the world? Rest assured that you have nothing to be ashamed of.

What you did, you did out of necessity. Even if you did it out of a sense of adventure, it still does not matter. What matters is you and me and the future. Relax, darling.'

'You mean you don't mind?' 'Of course, I don't. I am grateful, darling, that you decided to tell me about it. I am not going to reciprocate and tell you about my own past, but if anything crops up and you ask me about it, I shall surely tell you the truth, and I expect that you will accept it and know that whatever it was happened in the past.'

'Oh, Steve, you're so reasonable. Now I realise that I've been fussing and fretting about nothing." 'Precisely. Think of now and the future. That's all. If you've learnt a lesson from something that happened to you in the past, then that's fine, but don't keep dwelling on it. It isn't worth it.'

"Thanks, Steve,' she said, putting her head on his shoulder.

He drew her close. 'Evbu, will you marry me?' 'Yes, darling Steve,' she answered quietly, 'I will. I promise to make you a loving and faithful wife. You'll have no regrets.'

"Thank you, darling, you've made me very happy by accepting. I'm quite sure that I will have no regrets. I promise to cherish you as long as I live. I know what it will mean to you leaving your family and your country to come and live with me in my country, but I'll make it worth your while, Evbu, you'll see. You will never regret marrying me.'

'Oh, Steve,' she said, her eyes shining. 'We must break the news to my family as soon as possible.'

'Just a moment, baby. Here, give me your left hand.' He brought out an engagement ring from its box and slipped it on her third finger.

'Steve, you sly horse!' she exclaimed. "This is gorgeous! I simply love it. You thought of everything, didn't you?'

'Sure, I did, baby.'

'What if I had said "no"? What would you have done with the ring?'

'Pushed it down your throat, probably. Seriously speaking, I was confident that you would say "yes". I could feel it. Maybe I'm a bit conceited, but I knew that you would not fail to succumb to my fatal charms.'

'You're quite right. I'll go with you in rags to the end of the earth and all that stuff."

'Sure. Now, come here, darling, and let me tell you how much I love you."

Steve was an instant hit with the members of Evbu's family that were around when they visited. Nosawaru and his family were still away but Idemudia and his wife came over for a visit when they received Evbu's letter saying that she was bringing her fiancé home to introduce to them. Rachael and Izogie were also there and they brought their prospective husbands to meet Evbu and Steve. At first the girls were in awe of him because of his American drawl, but he soon won them over with his ready jokes.

His greatest admirer was their mother. After getting over the initial surprise that Evbu would be taken thousands of miles away from home, she waited on Steve hand and foot. She would make him tasty titbits in her kitchen, and bring him fresh fruits from her garden. He had to exercise vigorously in order to keep his weight down. She showed him off to members of her family and to her friends. Sometimes, though, she raised the question of whether she would ever see her daughter again.

Steve decided to put her mind at rest on that score. So, through Evbu, he explained to her that he and Evbu would visit Benin City every other year and that, if he got a good offer from a Nigerian-based firm, he would gladly come back to work in the coun- try. Evbu did not believe that he would want to leave his country indefinitely, but she did not let on.

Later, he was taken to Isi to be introduced to grandma. He and Evbu were taken to the Chief and elders of the village who blessed the future union between them. This was, of course, after the tradi-tional 'kola nuts' which the prospective bridegroom offered to them.

When they got back to Benin City, there was a family gathering at which Steve was presented to members, and he paid the traditional bride price to Evbu's uncle who had become head of the Isibor family. He would see that all members of the family got their share, no matter how small. There was great rejoicing and dancing that night, and the couple was blessed by the elders in the family, and were pronounced man and wife in the traditional way.

The actual church or registry wedding would have to take place in Lagos where most of their friends were, Steve and Evbu decided.

Next morning, they left for Lagos. On the way, Steve was pensive. 'You know what, Evbu? We may build skyscrapers and atomic bombs in the U.S.A. and in other developed countries, but you can never beat the true kinship in African families. I'm very proud, darling, to become a member of your family. I shall never let you down. I shall always cherish you as I promised your family.'

'I only hope that your family will accept me too,' said Evbu.

'No fear of that,' Steve assured her.

'What about your girlfriends over there? How will they feel about you bringing a bride home from jungle Africa?'

'Mother Africa, you mean? Don't worry your pretty head with such thoughts. Everything will turn out fine. You'll see. From what I've observed of you, you have a lot of confidence in yourself which other girls cannot shatter easily. That should see you through the first three months. When they see that you can stand on your own and not be pushed around, then they will respect you and rally around you. I believe it happens each time you move to somewhere new.

People want to find out what makes you tick. Anyway, you will fit in nicely, and I'll be the one to watch out that no guy snatches you away from me,' he added, winking. 'It would be nice to see you jealous, Steve, don't you think so?'

'Grrrrrrrrrrrr! Here comes the green-eyed monster!'

'Help!' she cried in mock horror.

Back in Lagos, they decided on a church wedding. Evbu had always dreamed of getting married in white and in the church, and Steve wanted her to have things her own way. Evbu was to continue working until Steve's next scheduled visit. Since that was going to be his last visit for some time, they would get married then, and then both go together to New York.

After his departure, Evbu set about the necessary preparations. It was very tedious, even with the help of Mrs Niyi, Kemi and a host of other friends. There was so much to do.

Steve arrived two weeks before the wedding. As usual he had a surprise for her. Evbu had gone to meet him at Ikeja Airport, and as soon as he came into the customs hall she flung herself into his arms. After the kisses, he gently disentangled himself and introduced the elderly couple behind him as his parents. Evbu was thrown into confusion for he had given no hint of their arrival in his last letter to her. She quickly regained her composure, however, and stepped forward to be hugged and kissed by the parents, while swearing in her heart to get even with Steve on that score one day.

'My, my,' exclaimed Steve's mother, hugging Evbu a second time, 'this is the only time my son has not exaggerated. He told me you are lovely and you really are. In fact, more so than he had described to us.'

'She's pretty,' concurred the husband while Steve grinned, and Evbu blushed.

'You'll have to teach me how to pronounce your name dear, Steve was impossible. He told me to call you 'Dawn', that that was the meaning of your name. Would you like me to call you Dawn?'

'I don't mind, Mrs Mayo, but...' 'Call me mother, darling.'

'I don't mind, mother, but I'd rather teach you how to glide over the 'v' and the 'b' of Evbu."

"That would be nice.'

'And now, Mum, if you and Dad would just step this way. I can see the company driver waving to us. He will take you to the hotel, and I'll ride along with Evbu in her car. From the glint of her eye, I know that she cannot wait to tell me off for keeping your arrival a secret, and I'd rather get it over fast.'

'Steve!' exclaimed his mother, 'you mean you did not inform the poor girl that...' Steve ducked as she feigned a blow and they all laughed.

When their friends got to know that they were in town, Steve's parents were not allowed to continue staying at a hotel. Several friends invited them to come and stay, and they eventually accepted the invitation of a close Nigerian friend at Ikoyi, whose acquaintance they had made while they had been in Lagos.

Evbu, on the advice of Mrs Niyi, spent most of her free time with her future mother-in-law. She informed her of all the preparations that had been made and asked for her suggestions. Mrs Mayo was pleased about this and they had endless sessions together. Steve and his father were pleased that Evbu and Mrs Mayo were getting on well because they knew that, though pleasant and helpful and kind, the latter could be difficult, and the former needed all the cooperation she could get.

The morning of Evbu's wedding day was warm and bright, but at midday when she began to get ready, it showered a bit.

"That means that your wedding will be blessed, predicted Kemi, as she arranged Evbu's dress.

'Really?' asked Evbu. 'With children or with money?'

'With both,' answered Kemi.

'Now, that will be nice, as I need both.'

'Evbu, do I look nice?' asked her sister Izogie, as she came into the bedroom.

'You look great, Izogie. Is Rachael ready, too?'
'Yes, here,' said Rachael, coming into the room.
'Will I do?'

'Of course. I'm quite proud of you both. You're so pretty.'

'Not as pretty as you are,' they both chorused and laughed.

'What about Mama? Is she ready?'

'Yes, she is,' replied Rachael. 'She's with the Edo women. She was surprised that you knew so many Edo women here in Lagos.'

'Not really. I know just two. When I informed them about my wedding, they went round with their friends and they all decided to buy the same lace material to use for the occasion. I thought that was nice of them since I'm virtually a stranger as far as most of them are concerned. Please give me that mirror, Izogie, I want to repair my make-up.'

'No, you must not look in the mirror!' cried Rachael and Izogie. 'It's forbidden!'

'Yes,' said Kemi.' it brings bad-luck to a marriage if the bride looks into the mirror while getting dressed for church.'

'How will I know if I look alright?'

'We will tell you,' said Izogie. 'Okay, then.'

'Evbu, my daughter,' said her mother, coming in- to the room, 'you look lovely. I wish your father were here to see you at this moment,' she added weeping.

'Don't cry, Mama,' said Evbu. 'I'm sure Papa can see us wherever he may be, and I'm sure he is happy for me.'

"That's true," said her mother, wiping her eyes, 'but very soon you will be many many miles away from me, and maybe I may never see you again before I die."

'You will surely see me, mama. You are still quite young and strong and New York is not even a day's journey away by air. Don't worry mama. Everything will be alright.'

'And you have Rachael and me around, Mama," said Izogie.'

'Yes, but you are not Evbu.'

"True, mama,' said Kemi, 'but they are still with you. Evbu will come home every year.

"Time to leave for the church now,' said Rachael. 'It's three-fifteen and the service begins at four. We will spend about fifteen minutes getting into the car and another fifteen minutes on the way, since you said the church is not far away."

'Well, it's about ten minutes' drive away, but we have to go at moderate speed so as not to upset the bride,' said Kemi. 'Evbu, what about your chief bridesmaid? The one from your office. I hope she will be on time. She's in charge of the bride right from the time she steps out of the car at the church. In fact, even before then.'

'Yes, but you see,' explained Evbu, 'Osarugue lives far away, at Ikeja, otherwise she would have been here. She promised she would be at the church at 3 o'clock, when she called here for last minute consultation yesterday afternoon. She's extremely reliable. You'll see, we shall find her waiting at the church.'

That was precisely what happened. Osarugue was hovering anxiously outside the church with the other bridesmaids when the bride arrived. She rushed forward to greet her.

'What a relief!' she exclaimed. 'I'm glad you've finally arrived. Steve made me nervous by sending someone out every now and again to find out if you've turned up. He and his friends arrived well before three o'clock. Evbu, darling,' she added kissing her, 'you look gorgeous! No bride can ever possibly look more beautiful! You'll make Steve proud.'

"Thank you, Osarugue, you look radiant!' 'Not so much as the bride,' said Tolu, Mrs Niyi's daughter.

"Thank you, Tolu. You and Bunmi look great. Aren't I lucky to surround myself with beauties on my wedding day? I only hope Steve won't be confused as to who the bride really is!'

'No chance of that,' said Bunmi, and they all laughed.

Just then, Chuck, Steve's colleague and best man, signalled that the bridal group was to enter the church. Evbu was astonished to see the church packed full. She trembled a bit, but moved forward smiling on the arm of her brother Idemudia, who was to give her away. Osarugue proved up to her task and fussed endlessly over the bride, the flower girls and pages.

The service went without a hitch and Steve and Evbu were pronounced man and wife, after which they went into the Registry to sign the wedding register. There, Steve could not keep his hands off his wife. He kept kissing her and asking for more photographs to be taken. Their parents and friends smiled indulgently. When they came back into the church, and the couple walked arm in arm down the aisle, Mrs Niyi's voice rang out loud and clear, 'Mr and Mrs Steve Mayo!' and some others took up the cry. Confetti was showered on the couple and more photographs were taken with various groups of friends and relations, and then the party moved on to where the reception was to take place.

The couple sneaked out of the reception after the bridegroom had made his speech. They stayed the night at Steve's hotel, and the next morning they flew to Jos where they were to spend their honey- moon of one week.

Evbu kept pinching herself to make sure she had not been dreaming. She felt extremely happy. Now that they were married Steve was even more attentive and kind to her. Whenever their eyes met, Evbu's heart was full of pride, love and joy.

And now, Evbu and Steve were in the bus taking them to board their plane for the United States of America.

Several incidents and pictures flashed through Evbu's mind-her family home in Benin City, her parents, her friends, special moments from the past.

She had been through quite a lot in her short life but she had been lucky. Yes, lucky, very lucky.

As the plane flew over Lagos, Evbu said in her heart, 'Adieu Jide, rest in peace. I've found happiness now, and I hope you're happy wherever you are.'

She turned and smiled at Steve, who held her close and whispered into her ear.

She lifted her chin. Yes, she was ready, ready to face the future with Steve. Everything would not always be plain sailing, but she knew that such a future would be good and full of happiness.